Carlos Fonseca

AUSTRAL

Translated from the Spanish by
Megan McDowell

MACLEHOSE PRESS
A Bill Swainson Book
QUERCUS · LONDON

First published in the Spanish language as *Austral*
by Editorial Anagrama, S.A., 2022

First published in Great Britain in 2023 as A Bill Swainson Book by MacLehose Press
This paperback edition published in 2024 by

MacLehose Press
An imprint of Quercus Publishing Ltd
Carmelite House
50 Victoria Embankment
London EC4Y 0DZ

An Hachette UK company

All translations of excerpts in this book are by Megan McDowell unless otherwise noted here:
Tomas Tranströmer, "From March 1979", translated from the Swedish by Robin Robertson;
Elias Canetti, *Voices of Marrakesh*, translated from the German by J. A. Underwood;
Juan Rulfo, *Pedro Páramo*, translated from the Spanish by Margaret Sayers Peden;
Marguerite Duras, *Writing*, translated from the French by Mark Polizotti;
Suicide, translated from the French by Jan Steyn; Rilke, "Seventh Elegy", translated
from the German by Robert Hunter

"The Musée des Beaux Arts". Copyright © 1939 by W.H. Auden.
Reprinted by permission of Curtis Brown, Ltd. All rights reserved.

A CIP catalogue record for this book is available from the British Library.

ISBN (MMP) 978 1 52942 261 0
ISBN (Ebook) 978 1 52942 262 7

10 9 8 7 6 5 4 3 2 1

Designed and typeset in Scala by Libanus Press Ltd, Marlborough
Printed and bound in Great Britain by Clays Ltd, St Ives plc

For Atalya, Rafael and Ari

Sick of those who come with words, words but no language,
I make my way to the snow-covered island.
Wilderness has no words. The unwritten pages
stretch out in all directions.
I come across this line of deer-slots in the snow: a language,
language without words.

Tomas Tranströmer, 'From March 1979'

A dream: a man who unlearns the world's languages until
nowhere on earth does he understand what people are saying.

Elias Canetti, *Voices of Marrakesh*

He has never been in a desert before, but he has imagined them often.

That's why every time he looks at the postcard he now holds in his hands, his first instinct is to see in it a portrait of the arid plain. Little does it matter that the photograph is in black and white. He imagines the tons of sand, the atmosphere of tedium, the feeling of emptiness. It seems there is no-one in the image, just a dozen lines meticulously arranged that he suddenly transforms into the empty streets of an old mining town. He sees the white drifts at the edges of the postcard and tells himself they are clouds. But then he starts to doubt.

On a closer look the white splotches lose their lightness and start to resemble heaps of salt. Just like that, the desert becomes a giant salt flat. The lines on the plain mark paths the cars full of saltpetre would travel along in this abandoned plant that reminds him, in a last twist of fancy, of the wrinkled lunar surface, with its craters and valleys, its archaic geometries. Only in that moment, when his imagination is exhausted, does he remind himself of what he knows: this is just a photograph of a dirty window, and where he'd thought he'd seen a desert landscape, a salt flat, or the moon, there is only dust.

*

The first time he saw the image, he remembered a documentary he had seen some months before. A feature on contemporary tourism that he'd put on by mistake, but which had drawn him in with its closing images. The final sequence, with voice-over narration, was a drone shot: the landscape of the golden plain around the Uyuni train cemetery. The camera slowly crossed the expanse until there emerged the ruins of what was once the first line of the Bolivian railway. Four thousand skeletons of abandoned locomotives that hark back to a glorious past, but today are piled up and rusting on the altiplano like the dry wind's captive junk. Strings of ghostly wagons that stretch for over three kilometres, sporting graffiti that the documentary's narrator read out in a slow voice, not without irony: "Such is life." "Here lies progress." Moving through that monumental junk heap like ants over sand were the hundreds of tourists who visit the place every day. The camera captured the scene of the pilgrimage, then continued on its way and left the cemetery behind. The voice-over fell silent, and the documentary came to an end. The credits rose up but the video continued, and behind the typography you could still see how the ochre shades slowly gave way to the white of the salt flats.

Now he is the one who is in the desert, but he keeps staring at the same postcard. Lying in bed, his back to the night, he turns the card over. The name of the piece and its author – *Élevage de poussière*, Man Ray, 1920 – are crossed out with a fine red line. In their place she has written: Humahuaca, Argentina. A simple gesture that transforms the work. And he thinks how strange it is to imagine a landscape when you finally have it in front of you.

PART ONE

A Private Language

No, there was no way to judge the depth of the
silence that followed that scream. It was as if
the earth existed in a vacuum.
                    Juan Rulfo, *Pedro Páramo*

Perfectly lucid to the very end, she had written in her letter, and she said it again now, out loud.

The words, coming from the kitchen, crossed the living-room on that December morning to reach Julio, who had sat in one of the armchairs furthest from the door to try and escape the freezing draught that periodically slipped in. Recognising the expression, he stopped rolling the cigarette he had in his hands and looked up. He saw no-one. Olivia had excused herself to make more coffee, and the only thing that moved in the room was the Italian greyhound that had jumped up into the chair she'd just vacated. He had the impression that they were acting out a previously rehearsed scene. Just last night, in fact, they'd been right here, sitting in these old leather chairs with three small lamps lighting the scene, telling the story that today she was recounting with variations. It was as if she were afraid he'd already forgotten it, or maybe that she thought repeating it was a way of understanding it. Two strangers who were seeing each other's faces for the first time, united by the trust placed in them by the fragile ghost of the mutual friend under whose roof they were speaking. Just like this, they'd settled in with a couple of beers from seven in the evening until well past ten, with the only difference being that now the morning exposed what yesterday had been only shadow.

In the daylight the house became more human, and the space took on a texture that before had gone unnoticed. The light entered obliquely from the west and shone on the wall where a couple of large black and white photographs hung. A picture of the Momotombo volcano yielded to the combative but endearing face of a young Sandinista in the early eighties. There were few personal photos, but you only had to take a look at everything else to sense the stamp of idiosyncrasy: a couple of reddish stones were displayed in frames beside an old grandfather clock, while further down, in a corner beside the dog food bowl, a dozen books on natural history were heaped in a patiently concocted disorder. Aside from a sombre arrangement of white daisies, there was nothing to suggest that anything had happened here. Under the flowers, placed between several terrariums, there were vinyl records, an impressive collection of old British rock LPs adorning the shelves that covered the rest of the wall until they ran up against the record player beside the window. Then, the gaze could relax and turn towards the outside.

There was the landscape, just as Olivia had described it. In the foreground, the twenty houses of the artists' commune and the couple of rusted bulldozers near the corral. Further on, down the hill, you could glimpse the place where the Río Grande intersected with the Calete and the Cuchiyaco. A couple of goods lorries, probably on their way to Bolivia, were heading north on the road, drawing the gaze towards the village of Humahuaca, beyond which towered the magnificent multicoloured mountains he'd only seen before in photos. Who would have thought the desert would be so colourful and cold? Accustomed to the screensaver idea of the warm, horizontal monotony of golden dunes, suddenly he was confronted with this: a mountain range where colours alternated vertically, with all the charm of a child's painting.

Poking up through the fog, the mountains displayed all the splendour of their strata, while higher up, in a clear, light sky, a sparrowhawk made its rounds, unwittingly imitating what had been happening since yesterday in that house that had again fallen briefly silent. He and Olivia, too, seemed to move in a spiral, approaching the heart of the story only to back away once more, perhaps aware that the truly important thing was to recreate, in that cold morning air, the absent shapes summoned by the words Olivia had just uttered.

"Imagine. Lucid in spite of everything," she rephrased herself.

At times she seemed to be translating into Spanish thoughts that had come to her in English. It was in those moments that the story's voice finally managed to blend with its subject, and he felt that the person speaking was not Olivia Walesi but rather his old friend, Aliza Abravanel. The same British inflections projected onto the Spanish, the accent masked but still there, the same will and the same momentum. Then emerged the exact tone that characterised the pages he had sat up reading until past midnight, in that manuscript that lay tossed on the breakfast table.

"More coffee?" she asked, interrupting his thoughts.

And along with the question, the evocation dissolved, as she refilled his mug and he, observing the tattoo that stretched over her forearm, understood the size of his error. He could not be hearing his friend's voice, not only because she had died ten days earlier, but because what was at stake in the story they now returned to was precisely the loss of that voice.

"Extraordinary, isn't it? Sick as she was, and still working," added Olivia, squeezing in beside the greyhound.

Backlit, dressed in the same olive-green jacket that had warmed him the night before, Julio nodded with a smile and returned to his half-rolled cigarette, first touching the pocket where he kept the letter that had brought him to this place.

The letter had arrived a week ago, along with the snow. Autumn had lasted longer than usual and winter dawdled until well into December. But it finally showed its face mid month, and along with the cold came that envelope capable of interrupting Julio Gamboa's useless ramblings. He was sitting before a paper on which the word *arctic* was underlined, biting his pen in search of associations, when he heard the three knocks at the door that woke him from the absurdity of his task. Why did he make those lists? Perhaps because, having reached that point where others might seek a new beginning in lovers or alcohol, he had come to think that lists were his way of maintaining order in a world that was escaping him.

"If I'm going mad, at least I have a method," he said to himself, as he saw the secretary enter his office with the mail in her hand.

Same as always: letters from the dean's office, magazines he'd never read, bills, account statements. Among so much routine he distinguished, however, an unusual envelope. *Humahuaca*: the address sounded so foreign, as distant and enigmatic as the sender's name, Olivia Walesi, which appeared under a postage stamp depicting a ravine full of cacti.

"I'm sure they got the wrong Gamboa," he said with a laugh, not realising the secretary had already left.

And he continued under this assumption as, sitting in his office facing the university campus where he'd spent the past twenty years, he read the beginning of the letter, in which Walesi introduced herself as a member of an artists' community in the northern Argentine desert. The following lines, however, finally dispelled his confusion. He recognised the name Alicia Abravanel with the kind of muted emotion we feel when we greet our childhood home after years away: a mixture of joy, wonder, and nostalgia. But he didn't want to give in to the games of memory. He put the letter aside and let his attention wander towards the students outside as they welcomed winter. It can take a long time for cycles to close, but sooner or later they come to their end with the most terrible precision.

Alicia Abravanel. He picked up a pen, crossed out the *i* and changed the *c*, which had always sounded so strange to his ears, back to a *z*. For the past thirty years, he had done exactly the same thing every time he came across that name in some cultural supplement or newspaper. He didn't feel like three decades had passed since their adolescent adventure. Time couldn't extinguish his urge to restore the name by which he had come to know her. Aliza herself, when they'd first met, had pointed out that detail, in an accent that only later would he recognise as unmistakably British.

"Aliza, yes, without the second *i* and with a *z*, not a *c*."

So, years later, when articles about her books began to appear and they all talked about a certain Alicia Abravanel, he couldn't help but feel it was all a simple journalistic error. No matter that he later read an interview in which Aliza reflected on her decision to change her name, explaining that in her case the Latinisation went hand in hand with another, more important decision: to adopt Spanish as the language of her novels. To him, she was still the same girl who had interrupted him one afternoon in the bookshop to ask for a copy of the book that would come to be the talisman of her youthful crusade against the world.

"Do you have *Under the Volcano* in Spanish?" she had asked, and then added, "by crazy old Lowry."

More than thirty years had passed since that day. Remembering her by her original name was his way of preserving an intimacy that had been born under the aegis of books and that now continued thanks to them, even as a letter composed in a remote Argentine province informed him that Alicia, his *Aliza*, had just died after over a decade of fighting an illness that had ultimately left her nearly mute, but that had failed to deter her from writing.

Perfectly lucid to the very end, Olivia had written in the middle of her explications of the writer's final project, and that was the phrase that finally managed to provoke in him the thrill of memory. That mention of lucidity, strange in reference to a patient with aphasia, unearthed another expression he and Abravanel used to steal from Lowry when they were teenagers: *perfectamente borracho*. That was how the protagonist of *Under the Volcano* chose to describe himself to the authorities – perfectly drunk. The phrase reminded him of how, at first, his alliance with the young Brit had been, more than anything, a rebellion and an escape. A way of fleeing his fear of not living up to his parents' expectations.

His father had never had much. Just a humble grocery inherited from a distant uncle, and a paranoia magnified by his precarious livelihood.

"One of these days the gringos are going to forget about us, and then we'll really be fucked," he used to say when the alcohol heated his blood.

"So you study hard, kiddo," his mother would add with a half-smile.

Convinced that cataclysm was nearing, certain that Central America would soon sink into the deepest chaos, they had pinned all their hopes on their two sons. His brother, six years older, was the first to disappoint them. Realising that school was not for him, he'd sought opportunities in the street that the classroom couldn't give him, and had the misfortune of being caught by the cops mid stickup as he and some friends were robbing a tourist bus.

Julio was only ten at the time, but the sight of his brother in handcuffs was a humiliation he never forgot. Having reached the age when children start to abandon childish things, he sought refuge in books. Timid by nature, he found a haven in their pages, never imagining that someday those same books would grant him an opportunity. Seven years later, when he received the letter offering him a scholarship to study in Michigan, he didn't know exactly how to feel.

"You should get out while you can, son," his proud father would say. "These parts are falling to pieces."

*

For Julio, though, it sounded less like an escape than like chasing someone else's dream. He was only a teenager, but from behind his timidity was already emerging the ambition of one who seeks to bend straight lines. A week later, he met Aliza.

If Michigan represented the world, Aliza embodied another possible world, far removed from his parents' expectations. For Julio, this young music fan who told of seeing The Sex Pistols and The Ramones live in concert, who swore she had kissed Sid Vicious, was the lighthouse that lit up an unknown and frightening universe. She was a blue-blood who at the age of seventeen had run away from home and the obligations that came with her last name to disappear in the dark streets of a Central American country, where the first strident chords of punk were only just starting to sound.

Among the pages, attached to a postcard with a paperclip, Olivia had included a photograph of Aliza. A profile shot of that face he had seen depicted in the press over the years, a face that gradually grew into the severity, character, and confidence that could already be discerned in adolescence. Her dark hair that contrasted with the white flatland, her aquiline nose, her exacting gaze. On the back it said: *Salinas Grandes, Argentina, 2008*.

Julio turned back to the blank page before him. *Aliza*, he wrote, without much thought. Below that, he started one of his lists: *Thomas, Cardenal, Williams, Parra, Truffaut, Naranjo, Bernhard*.

He saw her again, young and indefinable, on the sofa at his house in the middle of a Stan Brakhage movie marathon. He remembered her in a dive bar, reciting poems by William Carlos Williams while everyone around her watched, entranced, though they couldn't understand exactly what she was saying. He called up an image of her face from one long-ago evening when she sat at the wheel of his father's old van, crossing borders as if they didn't exist. They were heading for Guatemala, he recalled, and he tried to explain to himself why they had separated at the end of the trip. As he remembered it, the road trip had lasted longer than expected, and as the start of the Michigan semester loomed near, he'd had to return to Costa Rica in spite of Aliza's protests. He didn't think he had talked to her again after that. Their paths had overlapped for a moment, but after that youthful adventure he had set out down the road that would ultimately deposit him in this office, looking out at the northern snows, one professor among many, while she wrote novels about southern lands.

Much had changed in those thirty years. The anxious boy he'd been had managed to establish himself in a world that had once seemed terrifying. His first year in the United States had been hard: he felt terribly foreign and out of place on that campus, in spite of the scholarship and his academic success. He had suffered a deep depression, and only a French student he met at the start of his second year had managed to pull him out of it. Marie-Hélène, a freckled girl very different from Aliza, had made him see that when a person is far from home, nostalgia and memories won't get you far, and he had heeded her words, finally deciding to carve out a path by dint of forgetting. After almost three decades, this decision to only look forward was the foundation on which his comfortable life was built – a bedrock that had been set trembling by the letter's arrival.

*

Julio returned to the list he had just made: *Thomas, Cardenal, Williams, Parra, Truffaut, Naranjo, Bernhard.* This was the pleasure of inventories: to find order in memories where others would only see an arbitrary chaos. It was strange to think he hadn't seen Aliza in so long. That was why he'd been surprised to find the invitation written on the back of the postcard. There, after introducing herself, Olivia Walesi proceeded to ask for help:

> *Alicia asked me to get in touch with you, when it became necessary, and tell you of her irrevocable wish that you should be the one to edit her final manuscript, the novel or memoir (that will be for you to determine, as you know her better than anyone) to which she devoted her final efforts. I hope you can accept. We'll wait for you in Humahuaca, and I'm sure you'll soon understand why Alicia chose to spend the final days of her life here.*

A request that seemed like a mistake, or, even worse, a prank. It was odd, that suggestion of intimacy, the absurd notion that out of everyone, he was the one who knew her best. It was as if deep down the letter were reproaching him for his inability to remember her in full.

It had stopped snowing by the time he went home after reading the letter. The night stretched white over the yards adorned with sleighs and Santa Clauses. Foolishly, he expected the dog to come out to greet him, but he was welcomed only by the silence of the empty house and the remains of the scene that had taken place two days earlier. There was the half-packed suitcase, and beside it the pieces of the flowerpot that he'd unthinkingly broken the day Marie-Hélène left.

"See? Maybe it's a good thing I'm leaving. It'll give you a chance to reconsider things a little," she'd told him as she moved her things into a bigger suitcase.

Beside it, trembling and tiny, her dog waited in the crate. The original plan was for her to go to Madrid for her architecture conference and come back afterwards to celebrate Christmas, but the recent weeks had not been good ones.

It had all started arbitrarily, when, tired of correcting exam papers one day, he'd got the idea into his head that it was time to return to Costa Rica. He mentioned it that night to his wife, and Marie-Hélène's reply had been categorical.

"Are you crazy? We're not at an age to start all over again." And she'd added: "Nor can I see you going back. You're more of a gringo than anyone around here."

That answer had awakened a new sense of angst. More than angst – insecurity. He saw that perhaps she was right. There was little left for him in Costa Rica: even if he went back, he wasn't sure anyone would recognise him. Time had turned him into a foreigner. His parents had died some years before and the only family he had left were a couple of cousins he'd never been close to.

Frustrated with himself, he took his wife's words as an insult, and it festered over the following days. Until, in an uncharacteristic gesture of rage, he knocked over the flowerpot the day she left.

"See? Sometimes you behave like a dog," she said.

That evening she had called him from the airport. Marie-Hélène had decided to take the chance to hop over to Paris to spend Christmas with her family. He was welcome to come too, but maybe, she said, it would be better for him to use that time to relax.

"Go to San José, if that's really what you want. See how long you last."

His ambivalent reaction to her suggestion only proved her right. He didn't know what he wanted. In that sense he really was like a dog. Not a rabid or violent one, but a tame, domesticated dog like the one that had peered at him, confused and trembling, from its crate that same morning. A dog that couldn't find its way back home, precisely because it had been bred to leave the farm where it had been born.

The remains of that scene welcomed him the night he came home from campus after receiving Olivia's letter. The broken flowerpot, the wilted flowers, the suitcases with the blouses and stockings Marie-Hélène had left behind, the soil he had refused to clean up for two days. In that instant, the unexpected trip that Olivia Walesi was proposing seemed like more than an opportunity for rest. Humahuaca also sounded like a return.

Two days later an Italian greyhound had greeted him as the door opened, emphasising the distance that separated him from the house he'd just left behind. The same greyhound that now climbed down from the chair and crossed the room towards its water bowl.

"Isn't Clarke beautiful?" Olivia said. "He was the first thing Alicia looked for when she got here. She needed company and she found this puppy wandering through town. I think she named him Clarke in honor of a Scottish uncle who bred greyhounds."

Julio looked at the dog again. She was right, he was beautiful: he must be more than twelve years old, but in spite of his age he had an aura of confidence and dignity about him. So different from the confused and frightened little dog that had rebuked him from its crate in Cincinnati.

Then he looked at her. Yesterday, after nearly twenty-four hours of travel, the night and his exhaustion had whittled away at the contrasts. In the tenuous living-room light he had thought he saw the shadow of young Aliza projected onto her. Now, morning was making the differences clear. With her blonde hair pulled back into a thick bun, Olivia Walesi was far removed from the image he held of his friend from the eighties. It was hard to tell whether she was twenty or thirty years old. From behind her youthful enthusiasm peered the certainty of a person who's seen it all, and from a very early age. A gold hoop adorned the left side of her nose, while her right forearm bore a geometric tattoo:

"It's the lines of the strata in the mountains," she had explained the previous night, pointing to the dark picture window. The same window he had come to stand before again now, first picking up the manuscript that lay on the table, as if holding it would legitimise the tale of its genesis.

The story of the manuscript's origin was also the tale of Aliza Abravanel's arrival in Humahuaca. Eleven years ago, Abravanel had suffered a stroke. She survived, but the event left her practically mute, cut off from the words that had served her to create the eight books that had built up her reputation. Aware that the aphasia would only worsen over time, fed up with the pitying looks from her friends, she decided to get out of Buenos Aires. Take one last break. The memory of an old trip gave her a possible destination. She remembered how much she had enjoyed that trip she'd taken with friends to the north of Argentina in the early nineties.

"Words failed her, but not her memory," Olivia said.

Dismissing doctors' recommendations urging her to stay in the city, she reached Humahuaca with the celebrations for the new millennium just finished. In those years it was a torturous trip to reach Salta de Humahuaca, and tourism hadn't yet overrun its streets.

"She hated the idea that people would treat her like a gringa."

"Me too. That's why I'm travelling. To see if I can rid myself of this tourist face," Julio replied with a laugh.

Olivia ignored him and went on:

"Still, I think the work was also asking her to do it. As you know, in those days she was working on the last novel of the tetralogy."

Julio watched her gesticulate with an energy he'd first attributed to nervousness, but that he now thought was more from excitement. She came and went, from the window to the kitchen and from there to the armchair, then approached the handful of books piled beside Clarke.

"It makes sense, if you think about it, since only the fourth part was missing, the earth volume."

In the mid nineties, Abravanel had decided to take her work in a new direction. She left behind the autofictional narratives of her first five books and decided to dedicate her hours to a project in which human traces would vanish into vast panoramas.

"To record the human on its true scale," she had said in an interview he'd once come across. "To make it lighter, more playful, sporadic, like the silhouette of a solitary lion crossing an immense savannah."

That project, titled *The Human Void*, comprised what she called her four ecological novels, each dedicated to one of the classic elements. Those were the novels that Olivia was pointing out to him now, while Clarke returned to Julio from across the room in search of attention.

*

Aliza's readers witnessed the change during the nineties, how she renounced the fury of her first books. Her autobiographical impulses dissolved into large natural landscapes where human beings appeared only rarely, punctuating fictions that advanced through history at a tempo far removed from human psychology.

In the tetralogy's first novel, titled *The Invisible Border*, she followed the millenary contours traced by underground fires below the earth's crust, and from there she wove a secret plot that led to the figure of an indigenous child, deep in a Central American jungle, who swore he had seen the end of times in the shape of a thousand tongues of fire.

The second novel in the series, titled *Marine Currents* and dedicated to water, began with her childhood memories of diving on the Australian Great Barrier Reef, then later intertwined a chain of resounding historical images around the corals and breath, a kind of conspiracy of the depths that rose to the surface the day a child noticed that the waters had turned red.

From that reflection on oceanic breathing, the movement to the third novel, dedicated to air, seemed only natural. *Comparative Meteorology*, the last book published during Alicia Abravanel's life, was perhaps the most ambitious, as it began with a digression of two hundred pages about clouds, through which, little by little, her readers came to detect a theory about prophecy, information and prognostication. Little by little, everything came together and the plot became clear, tracing an enormous historical arc of more than two million years that led to a dystopian future scarred by natural disasters. Many considered that book, published one year before her stroke, to be the definitive consecration of a style that was already starting to spawn heirs and imitators.

"She never admitted it to me, but I suspect she came here to write the last novel of the tetralogy. I even know she wanted to call it *Strata*," said Olivia.

All that had happened before she came to this town, but in Humahuaca it was known that during her first years there, the writer had hired an indigenous youth to help in her efforts.

"Raúl Sarapura, the son of the man who was her guide on her first trip here."

They spent their afternoons together, seated facing the mountains, surrounded by the notebooks she asked him to bring. They gave no explanation to contradict the one provided by the town's gossips, who said that Sarapura took advantage of the mute gringa, squeezing her for money in exchange for filthy favours.

"The bastards called her the Mute," said Olivia, again placing the manuscript in front of him.

On the first page, written by hand, was the title: *A Private Language* by Alicia Abravanel.

The fixed ideas that would eventually plunge Karl-Heinz von Mühlfeld into madness had not yet completed their fateful arc – the one that would land him in a Swiss sanatorium, definitively lost amid the obsessions that once granted him such prestige, relating his life story between chess moves to a man who was my father – but in the only photograph that shows him and Juvenal Suárez together, von Mühlfeld is already wearing the white gloves that would become synonymous with his dementia. He looks tired, pale and withdrawn, quite unlike the brawny and intrepid man the people from the college say they knew, that overachieving student who finished his doctoral thesis in under two years and then decided to spend his third year delving into the muddy terrain of the Paraguayan jungle, with the sole intention of demonstrating the truth of his theories.

In this photograph he looks fragile, his face gaunt and wasted away, as if he has already surrendered to the fears that will ultimately bend his body as vehemently as he once bent over his work, as if he's already been imprisoned by the same fixed

31

ideas that years before had made him a renowned professor of anthropology. The indigenous man beside him, dressed head to toe in dark linen, looks elegant, reserved but lively; he has the imperious bearing of one whose solitude comes from being the last of his tribe. They are posing in front of a grand piano that perhaps in the past produced pleasure, beauty, even joy — seventy years before, that same piano had been carried by a dozen blond men through the swamps of Chaco, under the express orders of an illustrious philosopher's sister, who was convinced its chords would imbue the savage plain with Aryan grandeur. But years later, battered, its felt moth-eaten, it only endured as the ruin of a story so old that even its legitimate heirs would have considered it forgotten. If not, that is, for the morning five years prior when they witnessed the arrival of this exhausted man in the photograph, and they recognised in his face the importance of the story of which they had unwittingly formed a part. This man in whose face they recognised them-selves, but whose language they only partially understood. They were well aware that the years had doomed the German language to oblivion — or, even worse, to miscegenation and mutation. On that language's supposed purity, their forebears had tried to build the utopian village where they were still struggling to survive. In short, he was a man they would have dismissed as mad, if not for the simple mention of a name — Nietzsche, Elisabeth Förster-Nietzsche, to be exact — that was capable of reviving distant memories. And not even for the obvi-ous reasons, but because as children they had all visited the village museum and read about how, in 1886, Elisabeth Förster-Nietzsche and her husband Bernhard Förster led the fourteen

German families to found a small Aryan colony on the banks of the Aguaray River. Perhaps because they had read about that history and confusedly thought they recognised their own faces in the two oil portraits that hung on the museum's central walls, or perhaps because something in them still professed and swelled with pride at the ethnic superiority of which their great-grandparents boasted – perhaps that was why von Mühlfeld had only to mention the name Nietzsche for them to tell the story just as the oral tradition had recorded it in their collective memory.

And so, the villagers told that story full of mishaps that von Mühlfeld already knew by heart; he had travelled there precisely to hear that story's repercussions and after-effects. Enduring the heat of an afternoon buzzing with mosquitoes, facing the village entrance where an old German flag still waved, he heard how in 1883, Bernhard Förster had fled a country he considered infected with Semites, then crossed the ruins of a Paraguay left devastated and empty by the War of the Triple Alliance, guiding himself by a simple map where the shape of a triangle indicated the land where he could sow his fearsome dream.

Chasing a fantasy that would lead his own country to Shoah and ruin, that man of bushy beard and gloomy gaze, dressed in his traditional frock coat with an Iron Cross adorning the lapel, had crossed the muddy swamps of Chaco and the waters of the Paraguay River, dodging snakes, caimans, and midges, to reach the point where the Aguaray-mí and Aguaray Guazu rivers converge to form a fertile plain. Assuming the air of a prophet, he would baptise that savannah as New Germany. And if he didn't settle there immediately it wasn't from lack of strength or will, but because his ambition was collective, not solitary: to refound in those distant lands the civilisation that, he claimed, Jewish capitalism had corrupted. Without thinking twice, Förster turned and went straight back the way he'd come, through the Chaco swamps and the river's waters, to reach the ship that would carry him back to Germany. Once there, he set out on the propagandist mission that would find him in the port of Hamburg one year later, alongside the fourteen families who had agreed to accompany him on his journey towards a chimera that would defeat him after a mere three years. Beside him, a small, round-faced woman with a pointed nose and imposing bun, beautiful at thirty-nine in spite of a slight and well-disguised squint, waited hopefully for the arrival of the *Uruguay*, the steamer that would take them to America. That woman would prove herself the true leader of the project, and in her name – Nietzsche, Elisabeth Förster-Nietzsche, to be exact – there resonated the future echo of one of the greatest and most unfortunate misunderstandings of a whole vile history. That same grave error would in seventy years' time bring him, Professor Karl-Heinz von Mühlfeld, to repeat the voyage that those fourteen families had made in the spring of 1886. He was searching for traces of the woman who had contrived and twisted the writings of his favourite philosopher: Friedrich Nietzsche. This philosopher, weeks before his sister left for America, had made it clear that he disapproved of a voyage he considered absurd, and that he disagreed with its anti-Semitic funda-ments – the very same concepts around which his sister would eventually reorganise his ideas. For this round-faced woman would return to Germany, after the New Germany project had failed and Förster was dead. Finding her brother an invalid, paralysed by syphilitic dementia, she would twist his thought into the fascist currents that would culminate in the Nazism she later supported. He, Karl-Heinz von Mühlfeld, would grow up amid the ruins of that Nazism, unable to understand the history he'd been born into. Later, in reaction to that history, he would look to this forgotten commune for corroboration of his great anthropological theory: that all culture was the product of miscegenation and contagion. Over time this theory would threaten to transform into its opposite, leaving him prostrate in bed in a Swiss sanatorium, paralysed before a world he thought infested with microbes, unwittingly repeating the scene his philosopher had acted out on a Weimar balcony long ago.

But that would come later. In this photograph he still looks at the camera with attentive eyes, though something in him already seems to be moving away, withdrawing, hiding behind a body that perhaps was already starting to feel uncomfortable, irksome and clumsy. Beside him, his companion looks healthy, lucid, sympathetic. On the back of the image is written, in blurred handwriting, *With Juvenal Suárez, New Germany, Paraguay, 1965.* They must have been the same age: just thirty-two years old, more or less, but the ocean that separates the world of the healthy from that of the ill was already opening up between them. The gloves announced as much. It was his third trip to the town, but the first when he'd turned up with those perfectly white gloves, which make him look like a neurotic pianist – a kind of Glenn Gould of anthropology, my father would say with a laugh years later – liable at any moment to break out of the image's frame, approach the instrument behind him, and start to play the piano brought there by Elisabeth Förster-Nietzsche, who perhaps imagined that her friend Wagner's music would make her feel more at home. Only two years had passed since his previous visit, but much had changed: the hypochondria that some had started to notice during his second visit had become real, concrete as those ridiculous gloves he wore everywhere. He had first come to the town convinced that the failure of a colony founded on the purist ideals of eugenics would confirm his theories. Over the years, however, his own ideas seemed to have conspired against him, reducing him to a hermit who refused to touch the world. Little did he know that Dr Josef Mengele, who in the name of science and progress had carried out the most horrendous experiments in the death camps, had walked just a few years before through the streets of the town that now harboured him. He couldn't imagine that Mengele had hidden out among the same families who had received him so gladly – men, women and children who spoke passionately of a Germany they'd never seen, and who were equally ignorant of the Jews their ancestors had so detested – families trapped inside a past that defined them and among whom Mengele, carrying a Paraguayan passport, had surely moved with calm, certain that the town's history and President Stroessner's support would protect him from any betrayal. Karl-Heinz von Mühlfeld couldn't know that, and perhaps by the time of the photograph he wouldn't even have cared, immersed as he was in his hygienic phobia. An obsession that, years later, sitting across from my father as they played chess, he would describe as

"the spiral of thought devouring itself"

But I shouldn't get ahead of myself. In the photograph he still seems wrapped in a certain normality, to the point that no-one would notice anything strange if not for the white gloves and the presence of the indigenous man beside him, dressed to perfection and lending the image an anachronistic touch. It was reminiscent of photographs of those nineteenth-century travellers whose adventures von Mühlfeld had read as a child, whose exploits had inspired him first to study anthropology, then to set out on the series of trips that would bring him to this moment, taking a photo beside Nietzsche's sister's old piano, accompanied by an indigenous man whom the locals had started to call the Mute, since he never spoke, or if he did it wasn't in any language they knew: not Guarani, not Spanish, not Chamacoco or Sanapaná. All could recognise in that man's face the loyalty that would join the pair for life. Their shared solitudes more than once occasioned gossip and rumours, but von Mühlfeld wouldn't reveal their secret until the very end. Only then, aware that death was near, did he decide the time had come to tell the story of his solitary companion. That was when he sent for my father.

"They called her the Mute," Olivia said, and that painful allusion to a cruel nickname resonated with the story he'd read the night before. He intuited that if those pages on the long story of the New Germany commune also included a person named the Mute, it wasn't down to a whim of Abravanel's or a mere coincidence. Rather, it was because this posthumous manuscript was written in a personal key. Latent, encoded in the delirious wanderings of Karl-Heinz von Mühlfeld and Elisabeth Förster-Nietzsche, there was an autobiographical story. He had first felt its vibrations yesterday, when he set to reading the novel and recognised what, sitting across from Walesi today, he would describe as her *true style*: Aliza Abravanel's voice, exuberant and repetitive, wrapped in all her excesses. In this rough, unpublished work, the marrow of her prose finally became visible, and he thought he recalled her now just as he had known her thirty years before.

"A style in the raw," Olivia summarised, walking to the record player and putting on one of the old LPs.

As he recognised Tom Waits's raspy voice, Julio remembered an idiosyncrasy of that teenage girl who had managed to pull him from his youthful solitude. A slight tic: when Aliza was annoyed by the hair in her face, she would suddenly bite it and push it aside with a turn of her neck. Authentic style was something like that: a nervous twitch that might be invisible to a stranger, but without which our friends would swear they didn't recognise us. True style was unhygienic, dirty, full of those same impurities that Bernhard Förster travelled to Paraguay intending to eliminate. Yesterday, reading the first pages of the manuscript, he'd thought he'd finally seen her: the ferocity of her personality setting the rhythm of the prose by virtue of the repetitions that gave the sentences no respite, pushing the story forward purely on the strength of resonances. That punk style didn't come from the prose of Bukowski, Burroughs or Kerouac – the authors she had imitated at the start of her career, in autobiographical novels in which he'd looked for himself fruitlessly – but rather from much earlier readings that, Olivia told him, she seemed to have forgotten for years, but had remembered as soon as words began to fail her. A prose closer to Faulkner, to Onetti or Céline, writers she had forced herself to leave aside under the pressure of finding her own rebellious voice, but that perhaps she'd returned to when she understood that the time had come to rely on the voices of others. He imagined her sitting before the desert with the window open and the greyhound beside her, hands guided by the rhythm of the keyboard, aware the moment had come to return to her first readings and find in them a musical style that was something like a fugue – one that, like the river, would engulf the story she wanted to tell. A story that united two distant worlds, and that Olivia's voice now conjured up again with a simple expression.

"The Mute, they called her," she repeated, shaking her head.

And he intuited that the story had its roots in reality. Behind the name Raúl Sarapura, the indigenous man who'd helped her since her first days in Humahuaca, lay the biographical key that revealed Aliza in her more primitive state, inheritor of those two traditions that converged around New Germany. Jewish suffering meeting indigenous suffering in a ferocious game of doubles that included him and Olivia, just as it had included Olivia and Aliza, Aliza and Sarapura, the Mute and von Mühlfeld. A long chain of narrators trying to understand through retelling a story that was long and thin like a flame, able to devour everything in its path except for one name: Elisabeth Förster-Nietzsche.

"Yes, a style in the raw," admitted Julio, but Walesi, lost in the music, didn't hear him.

My father was only twenty-three when he was sent for. I remember well because it was the summer of '68, just a few months after the civil unrest in France in May that had finally awoken my parents to political life. My first memories come from those months. I must have been six years old, too young to understand the history that I would later read about, but old enough to know that in spite of his well-tended beard and the perfect diction learned at Cambridge, my father was still a child. Just a kid who feigned adulthood by way of diplomas, family and children. That year, he had finished his master's in sociology, which was how he first heard of Karl-Heinz von Mühlfeld, his trips to New Germany, his white gloves and his madness. Perhaps he was curious about that eccentric figure, or perhaps he was simply trying to give his career a push; either way, he agreed to translate into English a couple of chapters of von Mühlfeld's last published book. In its title – *Unreinheit des Reinen*, which he translated as *The Impurity of Pureness* – many said they could already discern the paradox that would ultimately lead its author into madness. My father never imagined that this translation would spur von Mühlfeld himself to summon him, when he realised that his phobias were winning out and there wasn't much time left to tell his final story.

*

And so, out of the blue that early summer, my father received the anthropologist's invitation to play a game of chess in the Swiss sanatorium in Zermatt, where, von Mühlfeld explained, he had decided to self-isolate in the hope of improving his fragile health. My father boarded a flight to Zürich a week later, and within five hours he was sitting before a perfectly arranged chessboard, the Swiss Alps looming in the background. The very stage for a turn-of-the-century novel, he would later recall. The man he met that afternoon was not, however, a tuberculosis patient, but a sort of premature hunchback, a body being devoured by the ideas that he had helped disseminate. Von Mühlfeld was wearing the white gloves he'd heard so much about, and my father thought he seemed to be speaking in sign language. The man was only a decade older than him, but already looked elderly: he walked with short steps, constantly aware of his surroundings, shrouded in an aura of mysterious silence like some kind of cloistered monk. Dressed head to toe in impeccable white linen, supporting his trembling steps with an immaculate mahogany walking stick, he resembled an anachronistic duke, an aristocrat marooned in an age that no longer believed in nobility. My father offered his hand, but the man merely gave a brief nod of recognition. And so they sat down at the board and over the course of the next five days, between chess moves, he heard the story he already knew by heart: the tale of trips to New Germany, of Elisabeth Förster-Nietzsche's commune and the Aryan dream that had foundered there. It was exactly the same plot he had helped translate in *The Impurity of Pureness*, but only now, sitting across from von Mühlfeld himself, did he understand the extent to which this man had engaged with the obsession that would destroy him.

*

He listened again to that tale that seemed to veer between the poles of comedy, tragedy and epic. A story that reached its apogee in March of 1888, when, in the Paraguayan spring, Elisabeth had crossed the commune in all her glory to reach the newly inaugurated mansion that Bernhard Förster had had built specially for her. An impressive estate that they would call Försterhof, a name born of their delusion. Listening, my father glimpsed the pathetic figure of Elisabeth, self-proclaimed queen of New Germany, digging her high heels into the damp earth, convinced that the echoing shots of the 21-gun salute were celebrating the rebirth of her race. Soon, the railway line would be built, her husband had promised, and with the railway's arrival the town would leave its isolation behind. They were ready to connect with the world.

My father listened to that story and tried to pretend he was hearing it for the first time. This initial boom was quickly replaced by desolation, deception and disillusionment. He waited patiently until the story reached the point at which, overwhelmed by debts he knew he couldn't pay, Bernhard Förster surrendered to drink. He knew that in this telling of the story, the railway still wouldn't reach those lands that were destined to fail. He could imagine Elisabeth Förster-Nietzsche alone, lost amid malaria and mosquitoes, trying to escape the suffocating heat that lashed the commune in mid afternoon. New Germany's coming ruin could already be foreseen, but its wake would extend far beyond the Paraguayan borders, all the way to that calm Swiss sanatorium.

Later on, reading my father's diary in secret, I would under-stand that this was the chronicle of an evil that did not obey chronologies, one that refused to end with the death of the man who had set it all in motion. As my father heard during those five long afternoons in the summer of '68, Bernhard Förster's death was just the beginning of a tale that threatened to outlive the last of its tellers. In von Mühlfeld's version, aware of New Germany's failure, overwhelmed by debts and drowning in alcohol, Förster decided to end it all with a deadly cocktail of strychnine and morphine. On June 3, 1889, a maid found him dead on his bed in the Hotel del Lago, where he had been living for months. Elisabeth Förster-Nietzsche, always careful, made sure to cover up his suicide. That year hadn't been easy for her either. Aside from the failing colony, an incident had occurred in January that would be recorded in the annals of philosophy, a scene that years later would fascinate von Mühlfeld himself, opening his way towards New Germany. The Turin police, on opening the door of the third-floor pension at Via Carlo Alberto 6, had come upon an unexpected scene: a relatively unknown philosopher was singing and howling and talking to himself while he fired off letters addressed to kings. Wearing his host's night cap as a crown, Friedrich Nietzche had begun his descent into the Dionysian madness he had so often lauded. Opposite the Palazzo Carignano, the self-proclaimed successor of the dead god was surrendering to the delirium that would hound him to the very end. Von Mühlfeld told my father how those memorable anecdotes had fascinated him from a very young age, marking the path that would ultimately lead him to Elisabeth Förster-Nietzsche and her vile Paraguayan colony. Born in Munich in 1933, inheritor of a war he was too young to understand, von Mühlfeld would find in New Germany the material foundation on which to build the anthropological theories that he would present in Parisian classrooms after the war. He was seeking a concrete way to cleanse his conscience, trying to convert into science what the impassioned ignorance of his forebears had ignored: that all culture is contagion, and purity is nothing but a doomed illusion. New Germany, that village lost on the Paraguayan plain, where white men spoke Guarani and indigenous men spoke German, would become his great obsession: if he was capable of narrating the failure of the Aryan colony, he thought, he would be able to redeem the unforgivable past that had scarred his childhood. Maybe because of the guilt he felt, he decided to call my father, out of all possible epigones. Possibly his last name revealed that his lineage held King David's inheritance, that Jewish legacy before which von Mühlfeld had tried to absolve himself in every one of his books.

We will never know his reasoning, but the fact is that during those five long afternoons in the summer of '68, my father listened to the story of von Mühlfeld and New Germany, trying at every step to understand that brief instant when an idea turns into its opposite and a man into his fears. Between them, the chessboard was the neutral ground where a story played out that to him, no matter its origin, could only sound strange and distant. Born just a decade after von Mühlfeld, in 1945, my father was nonetheless unquestionably a son of the post-war era, a boy who had felt the winds of history for the first time that very spring, in Paris. A child of Coca-Cola and Marxism, as Godard would put it. For that boy just recently become a man, the war was a distant and incomprehensible beast, a legacy of suffering that he had fought to leave behind, but that re-emerged as the anthropologist spoke. He told of how, when she returned to Europe in 1893 and found her brother incapacitated, Elisabeth Förster-Nietzsche had dedicated herself to the complex act of manipulation, distortion and editing that would ultimately forge the false legend of a Nazi Nietzsche. He told of how, once Förster and his fearsome dream had failed, Elisabeth would come to see in her brother the potential for a new idol. Her strategy? The manipulation of the archive that she would snatch from her mother's hands that same year, and the production of false biographies and profiles in which Nietzsche appeared as the pioneer of the very anti-Semitic ideas that he had condemned. Sitting before the glass of white wine he was always served, my father knew how to do what von Mühlfeld asked of him: keep quiet and listen to a story that ended along with the century, with poor Nietzsche paralysed in a rocking chair at Villa Silberblick, the old Weimar mansion that in those years his sister had turned into the archive of his work and a sort of museum where anyone who wanted could take a last look at the philosopher-cum-prophet. My father merely listened to it all and thought that the only real things in the world were coincidences and resonances, like the ones now drawing a clear connecting line between the figure of the mad philosopher and the man in front of him, and perhaps he was convinced that history was something that the will of men could invert, repeating in the key of farce what in the past was played as tragedy. He merely listened, and, hours later, sitting in his hotel room, he tried to transcribe all the details of their meetings in the pages of his diary.

*

For a long time, I thought my father should have burned his diaries. For many years I turned my back on them with the same fury with which, since adolescence, I denied my inheritance, my language, my past. Now I realise that those diaries were the only way for me to keep him close, even though his image in them was merely a fragile shadow cast over the figure of the anthropologist, in yellowed pages that seem full of echoes:

July 18, 1968

Today, when I entered the sanatorium, I found him sleeping in the rocking chair, and I couldn't help but remember Harry Graf Kessler's description of a moribund Nietzsche. The mighty head resting on his chest as if it were too heavy for his neck. Forehead furrowed, though his hair was still blond and impeccable, as was the shaggy, puffy moustache that was as voluminous as ever. Deep circles under his eyes, traces of an insomnia that was now giving him a rare respite. Further down, folded on his lap like in a religious image, were the hands sheathed in those famous white gloves. I remember how when I entered, for a moment I thought I was looking at a cadaver. Beside him, a very young nurse – so young that she somehow reminded me of my daughter – accompanied him, unaware that rather than caring for a patient, she seemed to be consoling a dead man. I found my way to my usual chair and felt a brief joy when I saw the chess pieces and the glass of white wine all set up.

At weekends of my childhood, when my mother brought me to the house where my father worked during the week and the adults sat down to lunch, I took advantage of any moment to get away. I ran through the hallways of the Hampstead mansion to his studio. There, thrilled by the adventure, I sat down to read his diaries. I locked the door with the old copper key and cautiously opened desk drawers until I found the leather-bound notebook where I read, in his impeccable handwriting: *Diaries 1968–1972, Yitzhak Abravanel*. I had only just learned to read, but there was nothing that could dissuade me – not the historical references, not the unfamiliar words, not even my own inhibition. Over and over I read the story told there in fragments, convinced that I would find his essence in those pages, the same essence that was extinguishing little by little, leaving him prostrate in a kind of lethargy not so different from von Mühlfeld's. "Yitzhak was devoured by theories," my mother would often say, and in those pages I sought an explanation for it all, convinced that this was a story of doubles not so different from the classic tales my grandfather told me at bedtime, like *Jekyll and Hyde*. I read furiously, not understanding everything but intuiting that the important thing was the shadow that loomed over the story's margins. Sometimes I'd hear noises and stop reading. Afraid of being discovered, I'd look out of the window and see them all sitting at the table: my mother and her friends, always gossiping, my grandparents and the dogs, my little brother, always crying. Adrift among them, hiding among the chatter, was my father, thoughtful and introverted. And I told myself that, yes, what the diaries told was a ghost story, and its true hero wasn't any of the obvious people. Not von Mühlfeld or Nietzsche, not Bernhard

Förster or Elisabeth Förster-Nietzsche. Not even my father. None of them cast a long enough shadow. The real protagonist was the taciturn character who accompanied the anthropologist as a silent double: that indigenous man whose face I had first caught sight of in a handful of photographs I'd found scattered among the notebooks, and whose story I learned years later was the true reason von Mühlfeld had called my father. Yes. Years later, when I finally realised that I shared a destiny with that man, I reopened the old diary, and as I read I understood that the anthropologist had summoned my father because he wanted someone to tell the truth about the man everyone in New Germany had cruelly called the Mute, without knowing his name, much less the truth of his dilemma. Then I decided to sit down to write his story in these pages.

2

The problem with the road, Aliza had written in one of her early novels, *is that it produces the illusion of a purpose that doesn't exist.* The sentence, with all its strength and poignancy, was finding him again years later, riding in a Jeep full of empty beer cans, tools, and old maps among which Clarke stirred anxiously. Aliza had never liked endings. She thought they seemed artificial and false, unnecessary cuts in a flow that, like the colourful gorge they were now driving into, didn't lead directly to any destination, but to that no-man's-land called the sea, or, worse, to the hysteria of urban chaos. Perhaps that was why the endings of her novels were always strange, something like the slow burning out of a candle. And so, Julio thought, when illness proposed a natural ending, Aliza had imagined her final work as an infinite Russian doll that would help her mock death through a game of mirrors, written at the same immense speed with which the gullies and canyons flashed by now. Beside him, a kid with a hoarse voice and tattooed arms impatiently took up the tale that he had left half told, and pressed the accelerator again in an attempt to beat the impending dusk at its own game.

"We're almost there," he heard the boy say.

The Puerto Rican youth was named José Ricardo Escobar, but as a child his friends had nicknamed him Elephant: he could recite the scores of boxing matches from memory just as easily as he now conjured up his own biographical and artistic wanderings, the path that had ultimately led him to that desert.

"My old man got to New York in the mid seventies, wanting to be a boxer. They say he was promising, until a rabbit punch laid him out on the mat and then in a hospital bed."

After the accident, his father had to settle for watching the fights from the corner of the ring, shouting out loud what had before been purely visceral intuition. José Ricardo grew up in that environment, haunting the Bronx gyms, convinced that someday he would be the one to follow in his father's footsteps. To his regret, memory and books came easier to him than punches. A pair of enormous spectacles had adorned his face since childhood, and his speech carried a certain rigidity and stutter that paired better with his myopia than with the salsa beats that inundated the city in those days. Nor did it help that he was the only one of his four brothers who had inherited from their mother, a second-generation Irishwoman, the red curls that would define him for life.

"Ginger Elephant, that's what the Italians in the neighbourhood used to call me."

And, unable to show his rage with his fists, he went back over the list of all the fights in which Puerto Rican boxers had defeated Italian ones.

Twenty years later, everything that had once inspired laughter or mockery fitted perfectly with the personality of this boy who now slowed down, left the gorge behind, and, taking a right, pointed to a high hill in the distance.

"That's where we scattered Aliza's ashes."

Julio looked at him again. Walking that morning among the commune's cabins, he had laughed to think how everything that once marked José Ricardo as a typical nerd now bestowed on him the air of a very fashionable artist: the round glasses took on a certain ironic tone that played perfectly with his curly red hair. He was the son of a clash of identities that recovered its exoticism once he was far away from the Bronx streets. Poised, without a trace of that stammer he claimed to have suffered as a kid, he explained how his complicated childhood as a shy, withdrawn boy, a bit of a freak, had ultimately led him to devote himself to books and art.

"I spent my days reading biographies of great boxers and drawing fight scenes. I never thought it would matter to anyone."

But life is fickle. One random day, an old painter from the neighbourhood had seen him drawing one of these fights and urged him to sign up for his evening drawing workshop. Heir to his father's prejudices, Escobar thought perhaps the old man was just making advances, but ultimately he didn't care.

"If painting is like boxing, I could stand to learn something from the experts," he'd said with a laugh.

In that workshop, he had met Olivia Walesi. He'd noticed her from the start. Sitting in one of the outermost chairs, she looked lovely and magnificent – and intense, from her piercing eyes down to the impressive sleeve tattoo that covered the left arm she sometimes leaned on, bending over her notebook to give her drawing the final touches. That night he'd spent the whole class sneaking glances at her, trying to understand the image drawn on her arm, feeling that the tattoo situated her on an ethereal plane halfway between reality and the world of the imagination. That's why he was surprised when she was the one who approached him after the class to invite him to a nearby bar, where a group of friends was meeting to organise what she enigmatically called "a few interventions". Weeks later, José Ricardo Escobar would learn that Olivia Walesi was the old painter's stepdaughter, and that he had been the one to ask her to include the poor kid with red curls in her nocturnal plans. But that would come after. That night, in a near-stutter, he said yes to everything and found out that by "interventions", Olivia meant night-time excursions downtown to tag the facades of bank buildings.

"That same night, someone handed me the spray paint, and, unsure of what to paint, I stuck to what I knew."

From that night on, every time he passed the corner of Rector and Greenwich, he smiled proudly on seeing the figure of the boxer he had idolised as a kid: Wilfredo Bazooka Gómez. Unexpectedly, art had ended up offering a way out of his shyness, opening the route that years later would lead him here, to the desert.

As it turned out, Olivia's dream wasn't to be found hidden in those graffiti, but in the great expanses of the west. Her idols were not Keith Haring or Jean-Michel Basquiat or Lady Pink, or any of the other graffiti artists who took the city by surprise in the eighties. There were other names that inspired her dreams:

Nancy Holt, Robert Smithson, Walter de Maria, Michael Heizer, all those artists who in the mid seventies had left the insipid claustrophobia of museums behind to venture into the vast western landscapes, where art could only murmur on a different scale. An enormous spiral made of mud, crystallised salts, and basalt, jutting out into the pink waters of Utah's Great Salt Lake. A field of lightning composed of four hundred posts of polished steel, able to conjure the spectacle of an unprecedented electrical storm. Three thousand yellow umbrellas lost among the distant valleys of California and Japan, urging us to think of a different kind of map, capricious and beautiful.

That was where art was to be found for Olivia Walesi. And she believed that she came to truly understand those works the day a friend handed her the first volume of Aliza Abravanel's ecological tetralogy, and, opening to a random page, she found a sentence that synthesised her attraction to the mad business of the land artists. She didn't sleep that night. She read the more than three hundred pages of *The Invisible Border* in one sitting, feeling that with each page she turned she was moving further out onto a shaky ledge. The next day she ran to the bookshop and bought *Marine Currents*. Sitting in a nearby park, she felt the anxiety of one who is sure she has found a living classic, that feeling of admiration combined with the breathlessness of knowing we are looking at greatness in the making. She held her breath and let herself be carried along by the rhythms and echoes of a novel that builds the way storms build, with a chaotic but perfect dynamic, until three days later she reached that final image, when the boy sees the waters turn red, and she felt the joy of being inside a paradox. She didn't think she had ever read a novel more human than that one, in spite of the fact that the human element in those books was a mere outline hidden in the eastern sands. And she didn't stop there. Two days later she sought out the third instalment at the bookshop and was surprised to find it hadn't yet been translated into English. Lost as she'd been in the immediacy of reading, she hadn't noticed that the books had been written by a Jewish writer of British origin who had adopted the Spanish language with the zeal of a religious convert or an adoptive parent. She was curious to find out who exactly was this woman who wrote hermetic novels in a foreign tongue.

A short internet search led her to the image of an imposing, solemn woman, whose eyes held a perfect balance between defiance and tenderness. Olivia entertained herself by jumping between photographs until she found one she thought seemed to show the author's true character. Dressed in a dark suit and tie and wearing a serious expression, the writer faced the camera with absolute confidence, wrapped in an aura of measured distance that suggested a hidden smile. A sort of contemporary dandy, Olivia must have thought, while she went on to read Aliza's biographical information: how she had been born in London, and at seventeen had set off for Nicaragua as a photojournalist, tasked with reporting and photographing the Sandinistas' exploits.

"Well, you know the rest better than anyone," José Ricardo added after a pause, aware he was talking to a man who had met her during precisely those years.

She never went back. She changed her name from Aliza to Alicia, and, starting from that minimal displacement, she built a literary oeuvre in Spanish that, as Olivia read, came from Argentina. The allusion to the remote desert took her by surprise and made her think of the artists she so admired. Then Olivia remembered the third volume of the tetralogy.

"That's why she thought of me. She knew I spoke Spanish, so I could help her read it."

Weeks later, when Walesi and Escobar finished the unusual process of reading and translation, they were not just a couple; they had also glimpsed the possibility of a shared future. The image of that writer lost in the deserts of the south tempted them to imagine that their destiny lay not in the euphoria of New York, but among those canyons into which José Ricardo Escobar's Jeep now drove further. Behind him, the greyhound shifted impatiently, as if he somehow knew that this steep road was taking him to the grave of his late owner.

That morning, walking with Escobar among the fifteen houses that surrounded Aliza's old home, Julio had understood the urge some people have to leave it all behind and start again from scratch. He, too, had been known to imagine such an escape and new beginning. He briefly pictured Marie-Hélène's distant face in mid fight, but the image of New Germany, Elisabeth Förster-Nietzsche's Aryan community, managed to distract him. The solitude of the isolated town on the Paraguayan plain had its echoes here, in this village Olivia and José Ricardo had come to just five years ago, following in the footsteps of a writer about whom they knew only what they could glean from reading her books and the scant biographical information available, but in whom they would place their greatest hopes, unable to imagine that the author was then constructing the long story of another commune, very different from the one they sought to found.

"We started to build the house there, without really knowing what would come later," Escobar had told him.

Clarke had speeded up as they descended the slope that separated Abravanel's house from the rest, and they watched as the dog ran off to enter through the half-open door of the one

Escobar had just pointed to. It was the commune's oldest. He and Olivia built it with their own hands once they had decided to follow their dream, packed their few possessions into a couple of suitcases, and finally traded in the New York chaos for the arid subtlety of Humahuaca. The greyhound still had the habit, left over from those now-distant days when only two houses punctuated the landscape, of going in the front door without waiting for permission. Not that it seemed to matter, thought Julio, seeing how Escobar did the same.

"Come in, don't be shy," he heard Escobar say from the living-room, and he tentatively entered that humble house from which emanated a murmur of voices.

The image on a TV clarified their origin. In front of it, lying on a faded sofa, a blond, gangly boy was intently watching a Colombian soap opera.

Maximilian Albrecht was the most recent artist to arrive at the commune. He'd come from Austria just three months before, bringing only a computer, a couple of ragged T-shirts, and a handful of programming books. He didn't even speak Spanish. He spent his days lying on the old sofa, trying to learn the local language between sips of beer and drags on joints.

"They say it helps to watch soaps," he explained, laughing.

So there he lay, smoking and staring with Austrian attention at the melodramas Julio knew so well.

"Some things never go out of style," he replied, shaking the boy's hand. He thought how his name, Maximilian, called up an adventure that had fascinated him since adolescence: the story of Maximilian of Hapsburg, who in the middle of the nineteenth century had become emperor of Mexico as part of the second French intervention in Mexican territories.

"Another Austrian lost in the south?" he asked aloud, but neither Maximilian nor José Ricardo understood the joke.

He was the only one to laugh, as he reflected that the journey of the forgotten monarch and his delirious expedition ended right here, in an austral desert, with this young man watching soaps. Impatient, capricious, his mind returned to the manuscript he'd been reading the night before, conjuring the lonely figure of Karl-Heinz von Mühlfeld lost on the Paraguayan plain, heir to a foreign madness that now surrounded each and every one of them like the very worst kind of plague.

José Ricardo Escobar again interrupted his tale of how the artist commune was founded, this time to show him the stone that told them they were at an altitude of more than 4,350 metres. A couple of vicuñas clambering up the rock face confirmed it. Olivia had explained yesterday that unlike the llamas to be found around Humahuaca, vicuñas and alpacas were more furtive, animals of the heights that tended to stay around the puna grasslands, the plateau in northern Argentina. They looked beautiful in the approaching dusk and Julio thought about taking out his mobile phone for a photo. Two taps on the glass distracted him again.

Outside the car window, a very well wrapped-up youth signalled that they would have to pay an entrance fee in order to go up to the lookout. He carried a mate gourd that he sipped from through a straw, and to judge by the colour of his skin and the depth of his gaze he was of indigenous descent. This was the first local he'd met since he got here, Julio reflected, while he heard Escobar chide the kid for what he thought was a rip-off, before eventually giving in.

"Come on, we have to pay now? That's new. You always end up as a tourist around here."

There were only twenty minutes left before sunset, and it didn't make sense to come all this way just to get lost in the dark. So they paid the twenty pesos the boy asked for and went on driving up the slope, until Julio saw the impressive view he'd heard so much about. It was undoubtedly the same mountain range he had glimpsed yesterday from the taxi, the same reddish peaks that would have filled Cézanne and the Cubists with envy, but seen from up high, its terrible nearness made it seem paradoxically further away. The mountains took on the arrogant air of paintings, always distant no matter how close you get.

Julio thought about the postcard in which Olivia had outlined her request, and about the game of expectations and illusions where the postcard image blended with real desert and dust. It made sense that Abravanel had asked Olivia to scatter her ashes here when the time came, here at the point where the mountain range became perfectly visible, like a photograph of itself.

As soon as Escobar opened the car door, Clarke zipped out to run through the brush that cloaked the mountain, disappearing little by little, off where the lookout point met the mountains at the horizon. It was summer, yes, but very cold, and Julio felt that every word he uttered was a waste as he struggled against the wind. Silent, shivering, he walked after the dog, while he heard Escobar in the distance trying to tell him about the origins of the mountains and of Aliza's decision to be laid to rest there.

"She said she wanted it to be here, she liked the idea of looking southward," he heard as he looked out at the view and again had the sense that he was immersed in a story that was familiar and foreign at the same time.

Escobar's anecdotes now reinforced that sense of estrangement. Julio had the feeling that he was intruding on the funeral of someone he didn't know, forced to carry on the legacy of a woman he hadn't seen for more than thirty years.

Almost every Friday for the past seven years, Aliza and the greyhound had visited the very spot where they were now standing. She and Clarke would wait there for Shabbat to start, then walk back down the path to the commune. In more recent years, Escobar and Olivia had brought her there.

"Her words failed her, but she still knew the scientific names of the local flora, or the different legends about the teasel flower."

Julio considered asking him about those legends, but he kept quiet. Everything in that place seemed like a summons to simplicity, especially the humble sculpture the commune members had placed there to pay homage to the memory of their matriarch. Two medium-sized rocks lay one on top of the other, facing the mountains. There was no name written on them and he never would have thought this was a kind of gravestone if not for the details the Puerto Rican had given him. According to Escobar, the two rocks were a perfect replica of the natural sculpture that the British artist Hamish Fulton found at the intersection of two long walks he had completed in 1976 and 1984. That work, titled *The Crossing Place of Two Walks at Ringdom Gompa*, was one Aliza had always liked, and, when the moment came, Olivia thought it would be a good way to pay tribute to the Jewish tradition of leaving stones on the graves of the dead.

Sitting beside the sculpture, Julio felt she was right: his friend would have liked the subtlety of that scene. Three decades ago, she herself had proposed a very long trip on foot, a sort of Central American crossing that would take them from the streets of San José to the ruins of Tikal in Guatemala. Her inspiration was a book by one of her idols, the German filmmaker Werner Herzog, who in the winter of 1974 had completed a three-week pilgrimage through the heart of Europe, walking from Munich to Paris, convinced that that sacrifice would help his old mentor Lotte Eisner miraculously recuperate from the cancer that afflicted her. Excited by the sharp surrealism of that walk, Aliza had imagined her own as a sort of peaceful resistance to the wars that were battering the region. Like the tightrope walker defying gravity with light steps, or the madman who crosses the street with eyes closed, she was tempted by the image of an absurd pilgrimage conjuring a brief peace in the midst of war. Aware that once her mind was set on something it was impossible to dissuade her, Julio chose instead to slightly modify the idea by emphasising a concrete fact: it was practically impossible to make that trip on foot, since it would take them almost six months. They would need a car. And so it was that in the summer of 1982, they had borrowed Julio's father's car and set off on a road trip that would ultimately separate them, and that now, three decades later, he was beginning to remember again.

My father thought his trip to the Zermatt sanatorium followed a mere whim: the temptation to hear the last words of a man who had once been a genius, but who now seemed doomed to disappear into the labyrinths of madness. Perhaps that was why he didn't know how to react when, on the third day, he found that the chess board had been replaced by a tape recorder. True to his British manners, he didn't comment on the change in routine. He merely watched as von Mühlfeld reached out his hand, sheathed in a white glove, and pressed the button that started up what he would later describe as

"the theatre of a voice doing battle with history",

a rough and hoary voice that alternated very soberly between words in Spanish and what seemed to be vocables in a remote language. Von Mühlfeld would later clarify the name and provenance of this dialect, but its remoteness and magic must have inspired in my father the same sense of anxiety and distance that struck the first men who stood before Edison's invention: the thrill of confronting a spectral object, light and fantastical. An apparatus, in sum, able to conjure the voices of the past and the dead.

Perhaps that was the experience he tried to record hours later in his diary, in two isolated phrases that were like lines of poetry:

"the theatre of a voice doing battle with history,
the silences of a language doing battle with oblivion."

Perhaps he understood then that the reason Karl-Heinz von Mühlfeld had brought him there was not exactly the one he'd imagined: it wasn't the chronicle of New Germany that concerned him, but something else. It was the story that emerged in the middle of that afternoon, with the monotony of those slowly spinning magnetic tapes, while around them, in a spiral, stretched the voice of a man who was patiently trying to inscribe on the air the memory of a language only he could understand. Later, my father would write in his diary: "More than the voice, what impressed me were the silences, the pauses, the lapses when nothing much happened but you could sense the hesitations of a man lost in a pursuit as titanic as it was useless." The same pursuit that von Mühlfeld decided to delegate to my father as soon as he realised his own energy wouldn't suffice. They let the recording run until the end, when the words finally ceased and there was only a floating voice that said: Juvenal Suárez, Dictionary, 1965.

Juvenal Suárez was the youngest of a family of five brothers, the last of whom he had seen fall prey to the fevers of measles. "*Mu unteva*," he'd heard his brother say, and watched him dissipate just like that, the way flowers or clouds disappear. At that time there were fewer than fifteen members of the Nataibo tribe and only Juvenal seemed to understand that the words held a sad prophecy. A few weeks earlier, an expedition of prospectors in search of gold had stumbled upon their Amazon village, and from that moment on the native population had fallen ill at an alarming rate. "*Mu unteva*," his brother had said, proud that none of the prospectors could understand what his words meant. They were words that Juvenal Suárez would translate two years later for von Mühlfeld as "this is as far as we come," speaking a brittle Spanish he had learned years before from the rubber tappers whose arrival had marked the beginning of the end for the Nataibo people. He'd been only twelve or thirteen years old then, and he had never seen a white man. He couldn't know, then, what the older people remembered: that those men were demons, thirsty for rubber and blood, capable of unspeakable atrocities. Much less could he know that during those years, on a distant continent, the world was laying its bets in a war that would destroy all but the heavens. Even the Nataibo, who had pursued isolation and privacy with such zeal, were not safe from that vile war. It was 1942 or 1943, and, when the Japanese captured the Asian rubber plantations, the allied forces had been obliged to return to the route that a century before had led thousands of men into the dementia of an unprecedented hell. Hope and a lust for victory were returning then, and the Amazon's waters were witness to the return of a monster everyone thought had been defeated. That was when a lost expedition of rubber tappers came into contact with the tribe, and Juvenal Suárez first saw the pale and pinkish skin of white men. In those days his name was not Juvenal Suárez, and if not for the old folks' memories he wouldn't even have known that they were men. In the following months he would learn it the hard way, on those rubber plantations where slavery came wrapped in the whisper of a strange language. That would be where he first heard the Spanish language that later, when the moment came, he would refuse to speak.

All that would remain of those years was a handful of words and the memory of the great wave of malaria that washed over them a few weeks after the rubber workers' arrival. That first epidemic, furtive and deadly, would take both his parents and one brother. Even more important, it took away the illusion of solitude and isolation that had surrounded the tribe up to then. So when the white men exhausted all the rubber in the region and finally set them free, the Nataibo decided to set off upriver in search of the peace that had now become synonymous with survival. After four days, they found a spot at a bend in the Tigre River that seemed remote enough, and they decided that was where they would seek the tranquility the rubber tappers had stolen. And they found it, or at least they thought so.

The years that follow are serene ones during which Juvenal cautiously watches the passage of time, aware that death, disguised as civilisation, is always hiding just round the corner. And so, one afternoon like any other, a decade and a half later, the hum of an aeroplane interrupts his nap. Rubber has been replaced by oil, and a US company – repeating a gesture as ancient as it is perverse – has decided that the only way to conquer the jungle is through evangelism. A week later they see the first missionaries arrive from Puerto Rico, bibles in hand. The image brings back the traumas of the rubber exploitation, the memory of his sick mother, the violent murmur of that language he has forgotten but that he starts to remember, with terror and fascination, as one more trauma. Those men and women don't want rubber. They are after something more ethereal but fearsome: the conversion of souls. And that conversion starts with a name. On the second day the missionaries gather the tribe, put them in a line, and baptise them with Christian names. He is twenty-seven years old, and a short, round girl with a face that inspires affection and tenderness looks at him and says that from this day onward his name will be Juvenal Suárez. She says it and he accepts – not so much by choice as by rote. After hearing the name so much he ends up recognising himself in it. Along with the name, the girl gives him another talisman: a Spanish-language Bible that he will translate to Nataibo in his free time, a process that will take years but will ultimately convince him that the white man's language is not necessarily the language of evil. This is a period of peaceful coexistence, of learning language and religion. It ends the day when, the missionaries gone, the Nataibo see an expedition of prospectors arriving in the distance and realise it's time to migrate again. The trip takes ten days. This time, they carry the weight of inherited bibles and the awareness that the jungle is filling up with enemies and intruders. They also, unbeknownst to them, carry the first outbreaks of the measles that will ultimately destroy them.

Later, Juvenal Suárez will summarise that time with a word my father will one day hear emerge from the tape recorder and copy into his diary: "Na'teya." Paranoia. From that moment on the Nataibo's existence will be marked by awareness of their imminent disappearance. Still, fifty members of the tribe remain, and none are willing to give up without a fight. Prepared to battle it out to the end, the Nataibo prepare their settlement as an impenetrable fort, they surround their village with traps and pits, even building a tiered surveillance system to warn of any enemy landing. They can't imagine that the enemy is already inside, in the form of a virus that will eventually reduce them to a handful of men forgotten by history. Just a week later, a member of the tribe has a fever, and when the shaman sees the reddish rash that marks his face, he knows there is no chant or prayer that can save them. And just like that, Juvenal sees the rash take the members of his tribe one by one, with the mysterious logic of contagion he knows so well, and he is convinced that his turn will come any minute. He watches his eldest brother die and then his wife, he watches his son and his uncle die. But it's at that moment, beside the brother whose whispered last words he will translate for von Mühlfeld as "this is as far as we come," that he understands that perhaps his fate will be even worse than his family's. He intuits, as he looks at the dying face of his last living brother, that perhaps the gods have ordained for him the misfortune of being his culture's only survivor. "*Mu unteva*," he repeats in anguish, and in the words he hears the stealthy echo of a private language.

Perhaps that was the echo my father heard again four years later, sitting before that Alpine landscape so far from the Amazon, when he heard Juvenal Suárez's recorded voice. It was a voice that held no traces of melancholy, no irony. Merely the objective diligence of one who knows his own fate and decides to accept it without complaint. Something in the timbre of his diction recalled the exactitude of a man merely going along with a pursuit that he may not believe in, but on which someone close to him has pinned all their dreams. "Juvenal Suárez, Dictionary, 1965", the voice had said, and my father could immediately divine what was at stake there: the hope for survival of the Nataibo language had been reduced to a couple of magnetic tapes where future generations would seek the vestiges of a culture that had long since ceased to exist. He also knew that von Mühlfeld's shadow loomed over that project, and it was that story, so full of contagion and solitude, of purity and impurity, that held the keys to the paradox that had led the anthropologist into madness.

Knowing my father, I can guarantee that he said nothing that day, merely listened to the unfortunate adventure of Juvenal Suárez, accepted the responsibility that secret entailed, and promised that on the fifth day he would take the tapes with him and continue the project von Mühlfeld had been unable to complete. Knowing my father, I can imagine that a certain reticence kept him silent, and only hours later, in the hotel, would he have dared to open his diary and write down the tale I'm retelling here. A story he would try to synthesise with a couple of phrases that as a child I read without understanding, but that today pursue me as the key to my own biography. Those phrases like fists that say

"the theatre of a voice doing battle with history,
the silences of a language doing battle with oblivion."

Phrases in which I now recognise my very self, aware as I am that time is short and words are failing. And I again imagine the scene from that summer of 1968 just as it was recorded in my father's diary: the anthropologist with his white gloves, consumed by the ghosts of theory that had turned against him. Opposite him, tender and innocent, my father, that young man who only months earlier had felt an enthusiasm for history for the very first time, but who now found himself dragged along by the demands of an intransigent past. Between them, the tape recorder – an object that anyone from his generation would have associated with music and sports – conjuring the voice of that man I would later see in photographs, the sole custodian of a language only he understood but the dignity of which he carried on, convinced that the true motor of history was a secret lost between languages.

Looking out over that mountain range where the strata blended together, Julio thought back to those pages and the long chain of inheritance sketched there: Karl-Heinz von Mühlfeld, heir to the madness of Elisabeth Förster-Nietzsche; Juvenal Suárez, heir to von Mühlfeld's obsessions; Yitzhak Abravanel, heir to the solitude of Juvenal Suárez, and Aliza Abravanel, inheritor of her father's passions. Standing and looking out at the desert, smoking a cigarette beside the two commemorative stones that acted as grave markers, the final link in that story became evident: the end was him, Julio Gamboa, heir to that private language in which Aliza sighed her final wish.

Last night, overwhelmed by the story he was reading, he hadn't noticed straight away that each of the manuscript's fragments was dated in the lower right-hand corner of the page. Only hours later, lying in bed and thinking about it all, did he remember having seen the dates, and when he consulted them he understood the complexity of the text in his care. Many of the fragments seemed to have been written before Aliza's first stroke, before the aphasia that in some ways the pages allegorised. On those fragments dated in the nineties, Aliza had inserted phrases by hand with a red pen to link the story with her own illness, which must have suddenly seemed like the natural backdrop against which to map out Juvenal Suárez's dreadful fate.

At first glance, the retrospective logic of it all confounded Julio, forcing him to rethink the structure of that text, the creation of which seemed to encompass more than two decades. He remembered the words Olivia had included in the letter inviting him to Humahuaca – "*Alicia asked me to get in touch with you, when it became necessary, and tell you of her irrevocable wish that you be the one to edit her final manuscript, the novel or memoir (that will be for you to determine, as you know her better than anyone) to which she dedicated her final efforts.*" And the question about the manuscript's biographical or fictional nature emerged, forcing him to reflect on the complex knot that tied this final work to his old friend's biography.

And the thing was that the Aliza who appeared in that memoir camouflaged as a novel was completely different from the one he had known thirty years before. The Aliza he knew didn't seem to have family or origin, only an uncontainable fury driving her to turn her back on everything. Never, in all the time they spent together, had he heard her mention this Yitzhak Abravanel around whom the manuscript revolved, much less Juvenal Suárez. Perhaps this was the biographical secret that pulsated in her early novels, the hidden truth that she always wanted to narrate, but for which she hadn't found a structure until illness turned life into fable.

He wanted to keep playing that game of association and memory, but Escobar's voice interrupted his thoughts.

"I don't know if you know about this, but it's only from here that you can see the sculpture Olivia and I have been working on in Aliza's honour," he said, pointing to a plain hidden between two mountains. "If the rain permits, it'll be ready in a month."

Escobar was right: only when seen from above did the work take shape. Julio stood looking at it for some seconds before he thought he understood. He saw the lines of a map, and deduced the reason why José Ricardo's car was stuffed full of old atlases and histories of colonial cartography. He recognised the outlines of the Caribbean Antilles traced in chalk or white paint, and, beside them, the earth where the artists had written, also in white: *Terra Incognita*.

"It's a reproduction to scale, drawn in chalk in furrows dug in the earth, of one of the first colonial maps, made in 1513 by Martin Waldseemüller," the Puerto Rican artist explained. And he added: "He was a famous German cartographer, one of the first people to use the name America instead of The Indies."

Julio listened attentively, curiously, but an idea ultimately distracted him. Trying to understand how that work would look from the ground, he imagined himself lost in a giant labyrinth, unable to find the all-encompassing viewpoint from which he could plan an escape. He was struck by the beauty of the work. He thought he understood the euphoria and discomfiture the first colonists must have felt, and he imagined wandering in that maze while around him the night grew deeper, just as it was doing now, and the map's outlines disappeared in the darkness.

"We'd better get going," he heard Escobar say.

He gave one last pat to the two stones marking Aliza's grave, and thought how the map really was an admirable tribute. A piece visible to all but that only she, placed at a precise distance and height, could understand. A work in a private key, he thought as he walked towards the others. The guard's silhouette made him think that the meaning of the manuscript he'd just inherited could be found right there: in the notion of a text that all could read but only one person could understand.

"A work in a private key," he repeated out loud, while he waved at the young guard who was approaching, stashing his mate gourd in a small backpack.

"Want a lift to town?" Escobar asked him.

The kid said there was no need, his ride would be there soon, but something in his reply rang false. As they set off back to Humahuaca and saw him slowly fade into the distance, Julio couldn't help thinking he was going to spend the night there. And he kept on thinking about that, in spite of the greyhound's barking and the voices on the radio discussing the gathering protests against lithium extraction. Nothing could distract him from that image of a lone kid on the dark mountainside, not even the explanations that Escobar started to give about the big party the commune would be throwing in two days to celebrate the summer solstice.

3

Standing in front of the mirror, razor in hand, Julio could hear the music from the party that had enlivened the commune for the past hour. Olivia had knocked on his door to call him down, but he'd excused himself, saying he would be there as soon as he finished reading some fragments of the manuscript. Little by little, it was becoming bothersome and personal, threatening to seep into his private life. Then, while he was bathing, he caught a glimpse of the source of his unease.

He had never been one for putting feelings into words. He'd often thought that this incapacity had led him to stay in the United States, where men bury the fears that stalk them beneath mountains of work. But now, finally free if only for a moment, he intuited that what bothered him so much about the manuscript was its mute insistence on recriminating him for his apathy towards the lost years. Stubborn, arrogant in their stealth, those pages reinforced the frustrating sense that the last thirty years had passed by without his consent.

He thought again about that Central American trip that ended with him and Aliza parting ways. The road trip had been his last rebellion, an exercise of absolute freedom with a purpose the years had obscured, perhaps because not even back then had he been clear on the precise goal of that singular pilgrimage. He tried to call up the discussion that had led to their fight and separation, but he only managed to conjure a distant image: he was driving his dad's old car, slowly crossing the Guatemalan border, until they'd reached the hostel where he said goodbye to Aliza. He couldn't remember much more – just his anxiety about the imminent academic year. He saw himself young and tremulous, back in Costa Rica, suitcases packed and ticket in hand, ready to set off for Michigan.

"The Good Student," he remembered Aliza saying with a laugh, during those months when he was debating whether to accept the scholarship.

A university grant that would set him on what his parents insisted on calling the "right path", but that after thirty years would leave him at the crossroads where he now found himself, unable to recognise the boy he had been.

"Hey, Escobar, buddy!" he heard someone shout.

Outside, the din of the party was another recrimination of his tendency towards isolation, bringing him face to face with the cowardice that lay behind the defeats that had ultimately led him there. Shaved and dressed now, Julio looked out of the window. A couple of bonfires lit up the landscape. Circling them like an accidental tribe, some thirty young people were talking and drinking to the beat of a couple of drums. He identified one of the drummers as Escobar, and he wondered what Marie-Hélène would think if she could see him there, adrift in a hippie commune, sharing the night with a group of young people who made him feel simultaneously as if all the time in the world had passed, and that there was still enough time to change everything. Further back, to the right of Escobar, he saw Maximilian, the young artist he'd met a couple days ago. He was talking to a couple of dark-skinned girls who seemed to be listening enthusiastically. Julio smiled to think that the Austrian was telling his stories in the accent of a soap opera heart-throb, acquired over the course of many afternoons training in front of the TV. The image, absurd and silly, finally relaxed him, and he told himself it was time to go out. To steel himself and brave the laughter of the crowd, just as he'd done some hours earlier when he'd braved the tale of Juvenal Suárez's laughter.

When the inhabitants of New Germany saw von Mühlfeld return in midsummer of 1965, they noticed the changes in his face, worn away by the hypochondria that would lead him first into dementia and then to his death. They also took note of the indigenous man who followed him everywhere like a symptom of that illness that was also announced by the ridiculous white gloves, but that now threatened to turn him into a hermit. On that third trip to New Germany, they almost never saw him come out of his house, and when he did, they heard him say in a very quiet voice, nearly a whisper, that the urgent nature of his writing, on top of his fragile health, forced him into seclusion and isolation. They were witness to how it was this indigenous man, impeccably dressed in dark linen, who did the shopping and helped von Mühlfeld with the cleaning. Seeking to clarify the situation, they tried to get information from the foreigner, but they couldn't get a word out of him. Not in Spanish, not in Guarani, not in Ayoreo or Aché. That was when they started calling him the Mute, and spread the cowardly rumour that behind the old mansion's closed doors, the pair entertained themselves with vile pleasures. They had no idea that this man was named Juvenal Suárez and that in his free time he laughed to himself at the ignorant gossip he heard. Much less could they know that his trajectory unwittingly imitated New Germany's own: two cultures forgotten by history, trapped like ghosts in a game of purity that not even the players could understand.

Among the photographs I found interspersed in my father's notebooks, there was one with the words "Calle Principal, Försterrode, New Germany" written on the back. In the afternoons I sometimes stopped reading and sat looking at that image: a dirt road, absolutely empty save for a dog that seemed to be looking around for a friend. It was clear the train had never reached that town, and that the *Hermann*, the steamboat Bernhard Förster had thought would connect the colony by river, had long since ceased coming. I looked at the dog and felt I was seeing a portrait of the solitude of a town history had forgotten, a commune where a handful of families blindly chased an epic tale that many would say ended long ago, but that in the middle of the seventies made room for Juvenal Suárez and Karl-Heinz von Mühlfeld.

As a child, when I sneaked off to my father's office, I used to read his diary entries about the adventures of that unusual duo and imagine – perhaps in an attempt to eradicate the consequences – that it wasn't real, but fiction: a light-hearted and ethereal tale like the extraordinary travels of Jules Verne that my mother used to read me at night. For a while, I would suspend the intuition that the secret of my father's sadness lay there, and instead surrender to the fascinating game of adventure in remote lands narrated in those pages. Over and over I read the story of Karl-Heinz von Mühlfeld, and as I read I felt that same ambition growing inside me, the passion of those men who'd risked everything to chase the faint light of a chimera. I repeated those strange names – von Mühlfeld, Nietzsche, Förster, Chamacoco, Sanapaná, America – and I saw how the path of a hunger and a destiny could open up on a rainy afternoon. I, too, would someday travel to those distant lands where tired men wagered their lives on becoming someone else. I, too, would cross the rivers of the Amazon in search of a lost tribe of white men who spoke Guarani. Spurred by those hopes, I ran to my room and opened my copy of *Around the World in Eighty Days*. In its pages, I had hidden the photograph stolen from my father. The photograph that showed the two of them – von Mühlfeld and Juvenal Suárez – posing in front of Nietzsche's sister's battered piano, perhaps already aware that the time to complete their project was running out. An anachronistic pair, vestige of a colonial world that many said had ceased to exist, but that inspired in me the most immediate of reactions: an intense fascination that little by little would turn into fear and later fury, as soon as I acknowledged that what was related there was not mere fiction, but the tale of lives that were intimately intertwined with mine. I picked up the photograph and searched it for traces of that chronicle that refused to end, even though it really was a story of endings, at its heart: the final years of Nietzsche and von Mühlfeld, Förster's failure, the disappearance of the Nataibo and the extinction of a language. To tell a story is to know how to find its ending, I would come to write, but in that story I read in secret, no-one was capable of putting an end to a plot that spilled over little by little, always asking a new narrator to take over. Photograph in hand, I felt – though I was still incapable of expressing it – that in this story, like in my mother's bedtime stories, the important thing was not the ending but its wake, the ripples left behind once it was all over and one could sit looking into a darkness full of ghosts. And that's how I spent my afternoons, until I grew tired and convinced myself once again that it was pure fiction, part of a big novel my father was writing in his free time. Then I put the photograph away between the pages of the Jules Verne book and I went out to play with my little brother, blissful in my ignorance, until days or weeks later my curiosity got the better of me and, once again, I sought in those images the confirmation that it had all really happened.

The truth is that none of it would have happened if it hadn't been for the series of coincidences in the winter of 1964 that led von Mühlfeld to learn of the Nataibos' existence and their imminent decline. In the long, cold winter months, unable to finish writing the first draft of the book my father would later translate as *The Impurity of Pureness*, oppressed by what he thought was a contradiction in his argument, the anthropologist opted to do something he never had before: give the manuscript to a colleague at the university. Two weeks later, the friend confirmed what he'd already suspected. That his theory, though fundamentally valid, was unable to explain a phenomenon that was becoming ever more common: the disappearance of cultures, ethnicities and languages. If culture is contagion, then cultures cannot disappear, but only transmute. Trying to explain himself, he mentioned the case of the Nataibo in passing. His words fell on deaf ears. Incapable of listening, convinced the book on which he'd pinned all his hopes had been ruined, von Mühlfeld excused himself, and once home he succumbed to the nervous breakdown that would isolate him for the next five months. The man who returned after those months of absence was completely changed, his colleagues all said, but he'd regained his confidence and was convinced that he'd found a way out of his theoretical dilemma. Little did he care that his face displayed the illness that some already suspected was stalking him, nor that his steps were starting to show the instability that very soon would force him to use a walking stick. As he would later explain to my father between chess moves, his return to the classrooms in the late spring of 1965 would be accompanied by a simple phrase in which he thought he'd found the path to a new anthropology. He was ushered along, as by an improbable guardian, by that phrase my father would write in his diary, in which sparkles the beauty of Karl-Heinz von Mühlfeld's genius: "In the passing from one culture to another something always remains, even if no-one alive can recognise it." He would try to confirm the validity of those words that same year, when he headed deep into the Amazon jungle. At some moment towards the end of those five months of isolation – months that saw him surrender to his fears and his phobias, months from which he would emerge devoured by hypochondria and nervousness – that brief phrase had taken shape in his mind, and his genius had seen in it a possible way out from the paradoxes that hounded him. That was when he remembered the name of the Nataibo, and he told himself that only a field study would be able to confirm the veracity of the thesis that seemed to have fallen from the sky. Two months later, as the passengers on the cruise ship *Alte Liebe* watched him board, they thought he must be some old aristocrat fallen on hard times: the impeccable white of his linen suit matched those immaculate gloves with which, prematurely aged, he held his American mahogany stick. None of those present could imagine that this was only the first of a series of ships that would ultimately deposit him a month and a half later at the mouth of the Tigre River, in search of a tribe that he believed to hold the secret truth of his theories.

We will never know what Juvenal Suárez thought the moment he saw, outlined against the river's waters, the strange figure of a man who seemed more like the reincarnated ghost of a nineteenth-century rubber baron than an anthropologist. Maybe something ancestral and instinctive made him think that this man was the heir to an ancient evil. Or perhaps, more earthbound, he merely let out a laugh at the pathos of a figure that could not look more out of place in the sad tropics. That first glance was all it took to realise this man was different from those who'd come before. Several centuries or even worlds separated him from the rubber barons, missionaries and prospectors Juvenal had known. This was the first blond man he'd encountered, and his eyes held a strength he had never seen before. Later on he would say it like this, in Nataibo: "Von Mühlfeld su intila ma'bela Uldu." And he would translate: "Von Mühlfeld didn't look; he thought." But that would come later. At that moment, most likely he merely peered at the newcomer in astonishment and laughed the laugh of a man with nothing to lose, full of freedom and joy, aware that for a man alone solemnity was an evil worse than any punishment the gods could send. He let the man row up to the settlement, and when he got a good look at him he understood this man was no danger to anyone except himself: his luggage held only books, and none of them was a bible. Let us imagine that when Juvenal saw von Mühlfeld arrive he had only to approach, point at the multitude of books the German was carrying, and hug his bible to his chest, as though saying, silently: we don't believe in pagan gods around here. Perhaps then it was von Mühlfeld who allowed himself to laugh, momentarily freed from the theories that seemed to so oppress him.

By then, only four members of the Nataibo tribe remained, and three were gravely ill. Two of them, the youngest ones, were suffering from malaria. The third was an older man who refused to speak Spanish, but if he had, he could have taken the liberty of saying what none of his companions would say: he was dying of old age. Around them, ghostly but playful, a pack of hounds seemed to be watching over the last descendants of Juvenal Suárez's tribe. Much had changed in recent years. Seeing that the population was shrinking by leaps and bounds, the tribe had been forced to turn to the medical services of a nearby town, and that step towards what some ignorant people might call civilisation had ended up profoundly transforming the Nataibo culture. Only the old man refused the change, continuing to wear the traditional garb he had worn all his life. The others wore T-shirts with US brand names, and their feet sported modern shoes. Around them, the jungle no longer seemed like the infinite refuge it had been in the past, but a mere ruin of itself. In recent years, nearby tribes had finally succumbed to western vices, and deforestation had laid bare the misery of a world that was now left in the jaws of a dozen wild dogs. It's no wonder that when he glimpsed von Mühlfeld coming downriver, Juvenal Suárez saw in him a possible escape rather than an enemy. That same day he asked von Mühlfeld to help him bring the two sick young men to the town with the nearest hospital, and when he took his leave of the elder tribesman, he felt that their goodbye condensed all his mourning for the world that had seen him grow up, but of which nothing remained but a muffled whisper. Two days later, a doctor informed them that the malaria would not recede, and Suárez, sitting across from that man who dressed so oddly, realised that he had no choice but to follow him to the end of his madness.

Three weeks later, seeing them arrive at the main entrance of New Germany, the villagers thought this was some kind of travelling circus: both dressed in linen, Juvenal in black and the anthropologist in white, they seemed like a couple of actors lost on the plains, not realising that this was in fact the very stage their jokes demanded. They watched the pair walk through town and disappear down the long, narrow path that would take them to the old Tacaruty mansion that von Mühlfeld had bought on his first trip from an old German who swore he was a descendant of one of the original fourteen German families. Then the townspeople didn't see them again for several weeks, but they could intuit that something in the professor's routine had changed.

And so, during the hot months of the southern summer of 1965, while the world turned its eyes to Vietnam, New Germany was an unwitting accomplice in that project by which von Mühlfeld was trying to save the memory of the Nataibo. Behind closed doors, isolated in that old mansion that harked back to an insidious past, they gave themselves over to the task that would lead to rumours and gossip, the real secret of which no-one managed to untangle until the day the anthropologist himself decided to show the tapes to my father. More than once during those months, curiosity would lead some local to approach the door of the house in Tacaruty in search of clues that would help resolve the enigma, and each time they heard only the monotony of a confused voice that was occasionally interrupted by a sudden laugh. The same laugh that my father heard three years later, when, sitting opposite von Mühlfeld, he listened to Juvenal Suárez roar with laughter after listening for the first time to a recording of his own voice. And my father laughed on hearing him, and he knew that in this hermit's project, in spite of the distance and coldness, there were also traces of humanity and charm. That day he returned to his hotel and wrote in his diary: "Von Mühlfeld is right: in the passing from one culture to another, something always remains, even if no-one alive can recognise it. Something minimal like what I heard today, when Juvenal Suárez seemed to be laughing at himself." That same laughter that my father would think he heard echoing two days later, as he wandered the hallways of the Zermatt sanatorium chasing a sound that he sensed did not bode well. He stumbled on the old anthropologist's room. He looked in and saw von Mühlfeld at the centre of a spider web of magnetic tape that he had spun himself, and he realised that the sound he'd heard was neither sob nor lament, but just the uncomfortable laughter of a young nurse nervously watching the scene. He knew then that his work there was done.

For two hours, sheltered by alcohol and music, Julio had managed to hide his shyness behind the peals of laughter that criss-crossed the commune and flew off towards the mountains. He even managed to forget the story he was reading in the manuscript. Flitting from group to group with a drink in hand, he listened to the stories of some of the people who had accompanied Aliza in her final months: a Polish artist who had come to the commune to dry out; a Mexican musician who'd been inspired by John Cage's wild experiments to put aside the sonatas and lose himself in the snarls of contemporary art; a Venezuelan artist who was convinced that the essence of art was to be found in the cave paintings of Cantabria.

"You get bored because you're shy," Aliza used to tell him.

And she was right. Few could know that behind his apparent patience was a simple inability to interrupt other people. And so he let them talk, listening to the artistic projects that had led them there. Works that ran from the construction of a hothouse of only red plants, to the configuration of an archive documenting the global circuits that traced the extraction, exportation, and consumption of lithium. Of all the works, none impacted him as much as the one that brought them together that night.

Because Julio had quickly realised that, more than a festival for the winter solstice, that night they were gathered to celebrate a singular work that perfectly depicted the ambitions that had led them all to Humahuaca. Olivia herself, leaving a couple of friends, had come over to explain it to him.

"I don't know if you've heard of *Sun Tunnels*, by Nancy Holt," she said as she handed him a whisky.

"I'd be lying if I said I had," he said.

And he listened as she told him how, from 1973 to 1976, Holt had installed in the desert of the Great Basin four enormous concrete cylinders in the shape of a cross, arranged so the tunnels perfectly framed the solstice in summer and winter.

Listening to the idea that had given birth to that work, Julio remembered the piece that occupied Escobar and Walesi's days: the lines of the colonial map that only became clear when seen from the exact position marked by Aliza Abravanel's grave. While the map called for a viewer at a precise position in the desert, Nancy Holt's sun tunnels called for an exact time. The paradox that the vast and anonymous desert allowed these games of precision and accuracy intrigued him. The story of the work's construction, as he heard it related then, ended up convincing him of its resonance in the strange plot he'd been living for a week now. The artist started building the piece in 1973, just months before her husband, Robert Smithson, perhaps the most famous of the land artists, had died in a helicopter crash when he was flying over Texas in search of a site for what would be his piece *Amarillo Ramp*. For the next three years, Holt drowned her sorrows in a collaboration with engineers, astronomers and contract workers that would ultimately shape the piece. At the end of 1976, she would invite the sculptor Richard Serra and the activist DeeDee Halleck to see it. They had arrived at dusk and stayed to sleep inside the tunnels, from which, punctured as they were with small holes that coincided with several constellations, they could see the starry sky. The next morning they awoke to see the sun framed by the concrete circles, their bodies inundated with light. Then, instead of staying there to celebrate the culmination of three years of work, the artist had wanted to demonstrate the true meaning of the piece, setting out to explore the desert along with her friends.

"As you can imagine, they walked for a couple of hours and then got lost. Holt herself ended up in the hospital, dehydrated," Olivia finished hurriedly, then excused herself to return to the merriment that was growing with music and booze.

Julio thought the adventure was brilliant. An anecdote that illustrated the need to mark a precise point from which the desert took on meaning. Thinking of Escobar and Walesi's work, remembering Smithson's death near Lake Tecovas, he told himself that *Sun Tunnels* depicted the process of mourning: capture for a brief instant the exact order of the void and then learn to let it go, let it gradually disappear in the open sky, while holding on to an instant that had been perfectly inhabited.

"Goddamn motherfucking fire!" he heard a man shout as he tried to extinguish the blaze, and the cry, accompanied by the laughter of two girls, pulled him from his reverie.

He looked at the scene again. Contemplating the joy and confidence of the artists around him as they took charge of the night, he told himself that they all still needed to take that final step, the one that Nancy Holt had taken so elegantly when she decided to set her own work aside to lose herself in the sagebrush steppe. All night long, something had told him that, beyond their individual projects, what was missing for many of those artists was precisely the bravery to take that one step further: to put the work aside and dare to lose it. Overly confident, they still lacked Holt's passionate senselessness as she disappeared into the desert, or Abravanel's as she disappeared into her writing. Too much posturing and too little courage, he thought, while he looked around and saw that the party was slowly mutating into a bacchanal. Seeing how the various artists were taking turns on the drums, he feared that soon someone would decide it was his turn. Anxious, he looked around for Clarke, but didn't see him anywhere. Still thinking about the story of Nancy Holt and her long walk through the desert, he decided the best thing would be to leave the party and set off to explore the nooks and crannies of the commune that these people, perhaps less drunkenly but with just as much enthusiasm, had built around the figure of his old friend.

He was just beginning to leave the music behind when he made out, against the silhouette of the darkened mountains, the shape of a man smoking. He stopped, startled, then recognised a silent and evasive boy whose solitude had caught his eye earlier at the party. Always a little on the sidelines, he contrasted with the other artists, so sure of themselves. He gave a slight wave, and the boy nodded. He took a drag on his cigarette and said:

"Almost like they're asking to be climbed." Perhaps aware he wasn't expressing himself clearly, he added: "The mountains, I mean."

That mention of climbing took Julio by surprise. Since his arrival in Humahuaca he had only seen the mountains from a distance.

"Yeah, or to be crossed on foot like the Incas did," agreed Julio, with a friendly smile.

The kid handed him a cigarette and introduced himself as Ignacio Acosta, and, when Julio asked him why he'd come to the commune, he began to tell of the long family journey that had led him to Humahuaca.

*

Acosta told Julio how he'd come following in the footsteps of an illustrious family member, recognising an outline of his own life trajectory in his forebear's wanderings and excesses. When he was little, his grandmother used to tell him about her uncle, Álvaro Guevara, an eccentric artist who had been one of the great painters of the European vanguard at the turn of the previous century, striking up friendships with Picasso, T.S. Eliot, and Gertrude Stein.

"One of those artists families talk about with both pride and distance, the way people always speak in retrospect of the rebel who manages to carve out a place for himself in the conventionality of their age," he said.

In his case, that achievement was accompanied by an anecdote that the Guevaras liked to mention in their after-dinner conversations: the fact, almost diluted into myth from so much repetition, that one of his paintings adorned the walls of the Tate Gallery in London. On his childhood afternoons in Viña del Mar, as he looked out at that bit of ocean that had once – according to another family rumour – inspired Whistler, Acosta used to listen to the story of how his grandmother had crossed the Atlantic in the seventies with the sole intention of gazing upon that painting that had brought so much lustre to her family. And at the end of the long voyage, which for the young Acosta conjured up images of distant and magical lands, she reached the museum and saw a painting that, she said, perfectly depicted a fish lying on newspapers, shaded in tones of ochre light that lent the image an astonishing singularity.

Remembering his grandmother's passion as she spoke of

the painting, Acosta smiled tenderly and emphasised that it was all the product of a misunderstanding.

"The painting by Álvaro Guevara exists, but over the years my grandmother's imagination transformed it. It isn't a fish on newspaper, it's a portrait of the poet Edith Sitwell."

Years later, when he dared to imitate his grandmother and crossed the Atlantic to lay his own eyes on the famous painting, he tried to comprehend how she could have seen a fish and a newspaper in that melancholic painting. The only explanation he came up with was that she must have got the wrong painting, must have confused her uncle's work with one of the still life paintings that abounded in the gallery's rooms in those years.

"Or maybe she did see it. That's the beautiful part: to think that over the years she swapped Edith for a fish and the rug for a newspaper. She kept a sofa and the general atmosphere of the painting."

The discrepancy mattered little: his grandmother's anecdotes had done their trick, awakening an ambition in the young Chilean that made him see art as the path into remote lands. If he was there today among the artists in that southern commune, it was because a stubborn intuition made him sense that his own footsteps were following the routes laid out by his distant ancestor's biography.

"Grandma was really great," he said with a smile.

His grandmother had died just five years ago, leaving him a photo album with a leather cover where he read an English title: *Sun & Shadow*. Depicted there in yellowing images was the story of the Guevaras just as he'd heard his grandmother tell it during long summers in Viña del Mar. That story began in the middle of the nineteenth century with the stubborn ambition of a teenager named Luis Guevara, who was convinced that someday work and destiny would grant him a mansion overlooking the sea, and it continued until, years later, the earnings from the transatlantic importation of wool made the brash youth's dreams a reality. *Sun & Shadow* was, in a way, the testament to that achievement.

"Then I remembered the stories Grandma told about her uncle," he explained.

One image in particular had awakened his curiosity. A photograph of Álvaro, eight or nine years old, dressed as a sailor, playing with his siblings in the shade of the trees that adorned the back yard of the family mansion on Cerro Alegre. At first attracted by the particularly luminous and almost ghostly figure of one of the sisters, he had digitised and amplified the image, and then managed to identify young Guevara's face.

"The same jaw and the same gaze that years later would captivate half of London."

The real surprise, though, had been to find a box camera on the boy's lap, newly visible in the enlarged image. He returned to the album's title, *Sun & Shadow*, and thought that, just as photography was an art of light and shadow, so too did his life seem to be the photographic negative of that boy's, who looked into the camera lens that long ago summer as one considers a destiny. He promised himself that, as a homage to his deceased grandmother he would devote his art to reconstructing the life that spread out over his own like a shadow.

*

"Other people like to trace their genealogical trees. I reconstructed the story told in *Sun & Shadow*."

It was, he soon found, the peaceful story of a wealthy family in Chile at the turn of the century. That peace was interrupted by a powerful earthquake that shook Valparaíso the night of August 16, 1906, destroying the Cerro Alegre house.

"That's when the photos start to change. They move from the port's crazy hills to the more rustic settings that intrigued me so much," added Ignacio.

Guided by his lifelong Anglophilia and convinced that Valparaíso was an unstable land, Luis Guevara decided to move his family to the city that had always captivated him: London. They began a long voyage that would first see the family crossing Chile north to south, through Araucanian territory. They spent two years there, recorded in countless photos of the Guevaras on horseback alongside the region's indigenous people, before setting off on the long crossing over the Andes to reach Buenos Aires. From there, in 1910, they would take a ship that would deposit them in London two months later. The same place Acosta would come almost a century later to study, thanks to a grant from the Slade School of Fine Art.

"You'll think I'm lying, but I later found out it was the exact same scholarship they'd given Álvaro Guevara."

Taking in the coincidence, Julio thought about Guevara's Araucanian years, crossing through Mapuche territory on his way to London. As the revelry grew louder behind him, he tried to picture that family on their epic crossing to the European metropolis, but his mind got caught up in imagining the cold they must have suffered as they crossed the Andes on horseback.

"That chain of coincidences gave me a project," said Acosta.

Leafing through *Sun & Shadow*, he'd had the idea to transform it all into an artwork: to track the coincidences, documenting the way his life was following in Álvaro Guevara's vanguard footsteps. A trained photographer, he had even reconstructed in photos many of the scenes Guevara painted in life.

"A rearguard for the vanguard," said Julio.

"Yes," agreed Acosta, "and out of all of it, the thing that most interests me was his sudden return to Chile."

And it turned out that the epic of his rapid rise in the circles of the London vanguard, which had adopted him under the weighty nickname of "Chile," came to an end in the early twenties, when Guevara fell in love with an irrepressible poet named Nancy Cunard.

"He wasn't the first and he wouldn't be the last," added Acosta, and he gave a long list of suitors that included Tristan Tzara, Ezra Pound and Man Ray.

Depressed, unable to tame the poet's joyful freedom, the painter had fallen into a creative paralysis from which he would only emerge in the middle of 1922, when he decided to honour his nickname and return to Chile. More than the phase of vanguardist euphoria, it was those silent years of the return to the south that interested Ignacio. The recovery of his native land was marked by an ethnographic phase in Álvaro Guevara's work. Years when the artist decided to self-isolate, returning to the land his family had crossed on horseback a decade before. With his memory set on those now distant travels, he sought in the Araucania an escape from the hardships he had suffered in Europe. Twice, he thought he found an answer: first in the image of incinerated trees that punctuated the southern landscape, and later, during his stay with the Mapuche communities, when he tripped on hallucinogens provided by the indigenous people.

"While his European friends were starting to experiment with opium, he found another escape in southern hallucinogens," said Acosta.

Between 1922 and 1924 he composed a series titled *Fleurs Imaginaires*, twenty-five paintings depicting imaginary flowers he claimed to have glimpsed in his hallucinogenic experiences.

That delirious project had impressed Acosta from the first time he heard of it, leading him to repeat the southern journey in an attempt to recreate photographically those flowers his ancestor first imagined. When he reached the Araucania he was surprised to see that very little of the native flora remained. The original landscape had been replaced by the monotony of eucalyptus and pine forests after multinational corporations had come to the country. An arrival that would have profound consequences, he soon understood, since those single-species forests were partly responsible for many of the ecological disasters that had battered the region for years. It had caught the young photographer's attention when he heard how those forest plantations were aggravating factors in the fires that threatened to raze the south of his country. He remembered the paintings of incinerated trees that Guevara had painted during his stay in the south. Since then, he'd been working on a series of thirty-six imaginary flowers based on that premise.

*

Without putting down his cigarette, Acosta took out his phone and held it out to Julio to show him the image of one of the flowers. A beautiful bloom, like a white rose, except that its petals were marked by small folds reminiscent of the aquatic beauty of sea anemones.

"It's not a real flower," Acosta clarified, "just a close-up of an exotic fungus that grows on eucalyptus trees."

"A parasite?" asked Julio.

"Exactly, it grows as a parasite on transplanted trees."

Thrilled by the unusual beauty of that false flower, Julio imagined just how exotic Juvenal Suárez must have found the figure von Mühlfeld cut against the backdrop of the Tigre River. Exotic but sublime, like one of those fungi cross-dressed as a flower that Acosta went on talking about now, as he picked up the story of Guevara with his return to Europe.

Listening to the story of the painter's final years, so far from the epic of mythical Chile, Julio felt that it was nothing more than the tale of a misspent life being gradually extinguished. His trajectory followed the arc of initial euphoria and late decadence traced by the inevitable exhaustion of all vanguards. He would have said goodbye to the Chilean if not for the fact that, as he reached the end of his story, he mentioned a final detail that renewed Julio's interest. Before taking his leave, the young photographer casually mentioned how, in those final years marked by tuberculosis and isolation, Guevara had dedicated the last of his energy to the elaboration of his *Dictionnaire intuitif*, a kind of lexicon made up mainly by defining a hundred French words that he found fundamental. A dictionary, he added, that his friends found open beside him on his deathbed, and that half a century later would lead him, Ignacio Acosta, to travel to this desert where they now found themselves, in search of a writer who had unwittingly repeated Guevara's last work.

"A dictionary, in short, like the one Alicia Abravanel made," he clarified.

The mention of that unknown project took Julio by surprise and spurred him to ask for more details. The chronology Walesi had given him had made him think that the manuscript of *A Private Language* had been Abravanel's last undertaking. Now, at the end of Álvaro Guevara's story, he mentioned this lexicon that reminded him of the aural dictionary of the Nataibo language. He thought Acosta must be confusing von Mühlfeld's unfinished work with one of Aliza's, but he changed his mind after what he heard next.

"At an artist's residency in Switzerland I met a curator, Federica Chiocchetti, who had just arrived after a stay here at the commune. She was the one who told me about the coincidence."

Listening to the details of the photographer's project, Chiocchetti had recalled the work that was rumoured to be occupying the writer's final days. She said Abravanel had thrown herself into writing a dictionary that she didn't show to anyone except one indigenous man. Fascinated by the coincidence, Acosta decided to travel to the commune to corroborate the Italian woman's information. During the four months that had now passed, he'd had the chance to meet Abravanel and confirm what his friend had told him. Unable to get information directly from the writer, since her health was very precarious, it had been enough to see a local indigenous man crossing the commune every afternoon.

"The guy was punctual. Exactly three hours later I'd see him take the road towards Humahuaca, where he got on the bus to Purmamarca."

Overcome by curiosity after a week of spying, Acosta had decided to stop him on his way to the town.

"He gave me a sullen look and told me the dictionary was still in a preliminary phase."

The man had excused himself, saying he had to run to catch the bus. But then, in a gesture that the photographer found inexplicably generous, he'd handed him a small card with his name and address.

"Raúl Sarapura. He lives over in the Salinas Grandes."

Julio recognised the name. He remembered that Olivia Walesi, two days earlier, had spoken of a Raúl Sarapura who had helped Aliza with household tasks and her linguistic rehabilitation after she'd arrived in Humahuaca. He remembered, too, the mention of the Salinas Grandes from the back of the photo of Aliza that Olivia had sent him, and he wondered if it wasn't precisely there, near Raúl Sarapura's house, where the photo had been taken.

"Did you go and see him?" he asked Acosta eagerly.

He was disappointed to hear that the young photographer, mainly occupied with drawing imaginary flowers, hadn't yet had time to make the trip to the salt flats.

"It's enough to know that the dictionary project existed for my reconstruction of the *Dictionnaire intuitif* to make sense," he added as he stamped out his cigarette.

Unable to reconcile the timelines, concerned about how that dictionary could force a rereading of the manuscript he'd been given to edit, Julio felt the weight of a sudden anxiety that he could only allay with two quick sips of whisky. He was going to tell the young photographer about the long history of his friendship with Aliza, but then the party distracted him: the Austrian he'd met two days ago running naked and shouting drunkenly in an unintelligible Spanish while the group looked on and laughed. He contented himself, instead, with smiling and asking Acosta for Sarapura's address. Tomorrow, once he had rested, he'd be able to solve the puzzle that Aliza had set for him in this final gambit of hers. He offered the Chilean another whisky, and, tired now, he let instinct guide him back to his room. He found Clarke sleeping on the bed, sprawled out like a medieval king.

4

In the early dawn, the acid residue of alcohol in the pit of his stomach forced him out of bed. Julio tried to ease the discomfort with a glass of water, but on his return to the bedroom, a radiant point in the distance woke him up the rest of the way. He thought he made out something flashing against the background of the mountain. Intrigued, he reached for his glasses and saw that it was just a shining spike of barbed wire reflecting the light, incandescent. He thought again of the dictionary the young Chilean had told him about hours earlier. The dictionary that, according to Acosta, Aliza had been writing with the help of an assistant whose name he now recalled.

"Raúl Sarapura," Julio repeated in an attempt to fix it in his memory.

He thought back over the events of the previous night to the precise moment when Acosta had given him the man's address. Careful not to wake the dog, he searched in his trouser pockets and found the paper on which the Chilean had written the information. Then, aware that his absence would be noticed, he wrote a note for Olivia that merely said, "Going to the Salinas to find Raúl Sarapura." He considered the various scenarios his brief escape might cause, but the excitement of discovering a work he hadn't known about convinced him the trip was worth it. Worried the dawn would expose him mid flight, he got his things and set off. The commune, barely illuminated by a bonfire winking in the darkness, confronted him with the immediate memory of all he had experienced the day before. Beside the dwindling fire, a couple of drunk artists dozed, surrounded by the remains of what had undoubtedly been a great party. Glad not to have to help clean up, Julio checked his watch. Only five-thirty. If he hurried he could get to Humahuaca before the sun was up.

The first rays of light caught him leaning against the bus window, at the beginning of the trip that would drop him off at the Salinas. Beside him, a fair-haired tourist was studying images of the landscape on his phone. The other passengers on the bus were all locals. Julio wondered what had led this man to choose, from among all the empty seats, the one next to him. Even if he didn't say so, he was bothered by that sense of foreignness that fell over him every time he came back to Latin America. That feeling of never really returning. An anxiety over belonging that occasionally even translated into grammatical errors and pronunciation mistakes, making him feel that, little by little, he was losing his language, and the last traces of his past along with it. Sometimes, during the short and sporadic interactions he had with Spanish speakers in the United States, he felt like he was missing words.

"A tourist everywhere you go," his wife had called him, laughing.

The words, unintentionally cruel, came back to him now as he sat beside the gringo looking out at the day that had barely begun, and he realised his wife was right. He felt like an outsider everywhere he went, which made him think of Aliza and her capacity, even before the novels and the name change, to adapt the world to her will. That bold passion for the foreign, the origins of which Julio thought he was coming to understand now after reading the pages of *A Private Language*, which had given him a new path by which to understand the teenager he'd met three decades earlier.

Karl-Heinz von Mühlfeld died on July 20, 1969. I remember the date exactly because it coincided with the long night when the Americans finally put a man on the moon. We had all gathered together, even my grandparents, in Hampstead. I was nine, old enough to know that a particular sense of expectation was focused around that event, the sense of an abyss that made us feel like the future was finally arriving. Long past was the war I'd heard my grandparents speak of in low tones. Even Vietnam and its sadness receded. I remember we gathered around the TV and for a brief second I had the illusion I was taking part in one of those adventures I'd read about in Jules Verne's books. A feeling of distance and lightness that was interrupted by an unusual call. The phone rang at about ten o'clock. A relative excited about the landing, everyone thought, including my father. So no-one worried and they let the phone ring. I was the one who turned my back on James Burke's scientific explanations and bothered to take the call. I answered expecting to hear my aunt's greeting, but I was surprised by a mild voice that seemed unaware of what was going on and simply asked to speak with my father. I remember how, when I shouted to him, my dad got up slowly from his chair, still focused on the TV commentary, and picked up the phone. He said the word "understood" three times, then said thank you and hung up. He went to the fridge, opened a beer, and sat back down beside my mother without giving any indication of what had happened. Only I, who followed him with jealous eyes, could know that something had happened, intuiting the thing that later, at dinner the next day, my father would summarise with a brief phrase:

"Crazy old von Mühlfeld is gone."

But that night he said nothing. He slowly sipped his beer as BBC commentators tried to explain what was happening, to narrate Neil Armstrong's light, silent, magnificent step that offered us a world. It was an instant that announced us as terribly modern, heirs to an open future, but for my father it would be forever linked to that call from a Swiss nurse informing him of the anthropologist's death. Understood, my father had repeated three times, one brief word to accept what the nurse was telling him from the other end of the line: in recent months, von Mühlfeld had been convinced his food was poisoned and had refused to eat, letting himself die of hunger.

He weighed thirty-three kilos at his death. Just two kilos more than me, I remember thinking, while I pictured Armstrong's monumental step and remembered a detail the commentators had mentioned: on the moon, everything was one sixth its normal weight. I made the calculation and it all fitted: my weight, the weight of moribund von Mühlfeld, and the weight of that first lunar footstep. Everything was wrapped in that arithmetic of lightness that led us in opposite directions: there where everyone else saw the weightlessness of hope and future, my father felt the weight of a history that refused to leave him in peace. A story that perhaps he thought had ended that very night, with Armstrong taking a solitary step in the darkness, but the after-shocks of which he started to feel as soon as he woke up the next morning. That night, though, he said nothing. Just drank his beers calmly, laughed along with us and celebrated during that long night, perhaps thinking that von Mühlfeld's death would bring the end of that chain of stories and failures that began with Bernhardt Förster and ended with Juvenal Suárez, including in turn the formidable biography of Elisabeth Förster-Nietzsche. A world that had been on the edge of collapse was now looking at itself from space and smiling for the cameras. A world that had reached the outer limit and decided to take one step further, and was now in outer space and celebrating that brave decision to leave everything behind and leap into the void. On that magnificent early morning of July 21, 1969, no-one thought of the past or of Nazism. Only my father, at midnight, contemplated the possibility that von Mühlfeld's death was closing a cycle that began in Paraguay and ended in Zermatt, a kind of historic spiral that, in the biography of that eccentric man, finally looked itself in the face and reduced to farce what was at first a tragedy. Nietzsche, my father thought, had been the beginning, and von Mühlfeld was the end. Then, I presume, he stopped think-ing. Beer in hand, it was enough to gaze at Armstrong's lightness to know he was living in a world one step beyond the end.

They say that astronauts, after long and solitary periods in space, tend to suffer from an illness that psychologists call solipsism syndrome. On returning to earth, many say they experience the feeling that nothing is real beyond their own minds. Lengthy stays in space – deep in the delirious experience of seeing the planet reduced to a small marble floating in the vastness – end up alienating them from the world. In the months after that historic July 21, I felt as if my father suffered something similar to that malady. While everyone else went on with their lives, heartened by the recent conquest of space, he withdrew into himself, coiled around a secret he shared with no-one save his diary, never imagining that I would read it days later. That's the only way I could know of the affliction that plagued him, the mourning that preoccupied him since the death of that man who in a mere five days had managed to become a kind of mentor. With von Mühlfeld dead, my father came to obsess over Juvenal Suárez and the story of New Germany. Tormented by the scene he'd witnessed in Zermatt, he felt that with the anthropologist's death and the destruction of the tapes, this perhaps useless but magnificent project to which von Mühlfeld had dedicated his final days would be relegated to oblivion. To take up work on the *Dictionary*, as he called it, became his great obsession in those days. More than once, in that time, I saw him sitting on the patio, whisky in hand, contemplating one of those long English summer sunsets, and I knew he was secretly thinking of those lands and the figure of Juvenal Suárez lost amid the poor heirs of Elisabeth Förster-Nietzsche's madness. Each time, I ran to hug and kiss him, afraid that one day he would set off for those lands that seemed to me more distant and weightless than the moon itself.

My kisses served little. In August, my father announced that he planned to travel to America for some months. Two weeks later, we went to see him off at Heathrow, and we watched him board the plane that would take him first to New York and later to Brazil, where he would board the ship to Paraguay. There is a photograph that shows him getting on the plane, smiling for us. My mother took it with the Kodak Instamatic. He looks happy and hopeful. He is waving with his left hand, while further off, in a quadrant of the image that seems to be hiding, his right hand grasps the dark suitcase holding the tape recorder he had bought that summer. An Ampex 960, identical to the one he'd seen in Zermatt. Just ten days earlier, my brother and I had watched him come home with the case and we'd intuited that it held some kind of toy. We weren't wrong. In the following days we watched him play with the recorder, and we suspected that this machine was turning my father back into the young man we'd once known. A man who laughed again as he listened to his own distorted voice. A certain optimism marked the weeks leading up to the trip, a certain hopefulness that by picking up the deceased anthropologist's project, he would be capable of reversing a story that already seemed doomed to play out in a tragic key.

And so we watched him leave, hoping that the man who returned to us would be a new one, full of life and energy. I remember how during those months, in the absence of the diary where I could read his secrets, I imagined him crossing over southern lands. From time to time my mother would receive a telegram, but it was always minimal, lacking the details I needed to light up my imagination. One telegram might say only, "Finally in Asunción, everything in order. Love to Aliza and Daniel," but I would make sure to fill in the blank spaces: I'd imagine my father in that city he knew so little about, tape recorder in hand, travelling across those swamps I'd read all about, convinced that his steps would redeem von Mühlfeld's madness. I saw him finally in New Germany, walking amid the ruins of a town that had once housed Mengele himself, but that now welcomed a man named Yitzhak Abravanel: a Jew who was unwittingly retaking his place in a past that my grandparents had struggled to leave behind. Repeating the past is a way of doing it justice, my grandfather would say in those days, and I, not yet understanding what the words implied, imagined my father as a secret hero. We had only to wait: one day he would return from those distant austral lands and I could secretly read the record of his feats and adventures in that town where the legacy of Nazism was finally disappearing among peals of laughter from the last of the Nataibo.

The man who returned two months later didn't seem to have had any experience at all. Quieter than before, my father had lost the last of the confidence that had brought him so much success. He wavered in his ideas, he stuttered when he spoke. He was, in sum, like a man who'd suddenly felt the ground tremble beneath his feet. He started to spend more time in his studio in Hampstead, and all we could do was look on from afar. The Paraguayans got his tongue, my grandmother said, and she was right. Turned inward, distant, he seemed to have aged a decade. I remember what bothered me most was the lack of diary entries. In the absence of first-hand stories, I ran to the diary in search of explanations, but I didn't find much. Just a page where he had jotted down von Mühlfeld's famous thesis – "In the passing from one culture to another, something always remains, even if no-one alive can recognise it" – and a handful of photos that gazed at me mutely from a distance.

In one of them I saw a pasture where an attentive eye could make out the silhouette of a big house in ruins. In front of it someone had hung a sign that read: Luisa N. De Förster. I remember it took me some time to recognise that this Luisa was none other than Elisabeth, and the solitary N was none other than Nietzsche. In those parts, the philosopher's name meant little. All that mattered was the vitality of the nature that bit by bit threatened to swallow the frightful Aryan dream that had begun there. Little remained of the grand airs that had once distinguished the old Försterhof mansion. Not even the decrepit piano broke up that landscape where the only thing that seemed capable of movement was a pair of pigs under the orange trees. Not even Wagner's music could stand up to the stubborn passage of time and those relentless termites that devoured all, even my father's own voice.

Years later, reading the series of articles he published, I would understand the reason for his silence. I'd understand that the man who returned to London in the winter of 1970 was one who had finally come face to face with the limitations of his will. Heir to opulence, son of a decade that strove to deny the past, he seemed only now to comprehend that some stories refuse to bend to our desires. I read how the version of Juvenal Suárez that my father saw in the streets of New Germany turned out to be very different from the one von Mühlfeld had depicted. Ensconced in the ruinous Tacaruty mansion, surrounded by stray dogs, Juvenal Suárez had decided to live out his days in the company of alcohol. Long gone was the elegance of the man dressed in impeccable black linen I'd seen in the photo I stole from my father. Drunk, he refused to speak Spanish, sunk deep in an endless monologue that only he could understand and the code to which he refused to share, even when my father took out the tape recorder, placed it before him, and begged him to return to the project he'd begun with the anthropologist. Of all the Nataibo culture, all of it, the only thing that would remain was the imperious and alcoholic ramblings of a man determined to carry his people's dignity to his grave.

Many times, over the years that followed that trip, I thought that voice hid the key that would someday return to us the father we had known as children. I would sneak down to the garage where he thought he'd safely hidden the tape recorder, and I'd press play and sit down to listen to Juvenal Suárez's hoarse voice. More than once I felt that the fury concentrated in the diatribe of this final speaker was precisely my own fury, the solitude of a teenager feeling ever more alienated from the world she'd been born into, a universe of luxuries that in those years I began to leave behind, going deeper into the world of punk music, which was just beginning to emerge. There, in the strident chords and shouted lyrics, I looked for the key that would help me understand the fury of that voice that was mine without being mine, until, soon after I turned seventeen, I realised that little remained for me in England. Around that time, I read about the Sandinista revolution, and something in me seemed to recognise Nicaragua as a possible escape. I picked up my camera, convinced a photojournalism agency to give me a job reporting on the conflict, and a week later I told my parents I wouldn't be going to Cambridge, but to Managua. I barely heard my mother's protests. Three weeks later, a plane carried me towards that continent from which my father had returned so changed. His diaries were hidden in my backpack, and in them the long history of New Germany, von Mühlfeld, and Juvenal Suárez. I'd stolen them that week, well aware that in spite of the hatred I now felt for them, we all have to confront our fears one day. And so it was: I didn't open them for years, until the day a doctor told me of the illness that was threatening to steal my speech, and I remembered the laughter of the last of the Nataibo.

Leaning against the bus window, Julio let his mind wander as he watched the landscape evolve: a singular progression by which the initial multi-coloured mountains gave way to teasel fields, then to the shrubs that punctuated the area around the salt flats.

"People call those shakers," a local youth told him, going on to explain that very few animals lived around there, since the composition of the earth made the shrubs highly poisonous.

"Sometimes the dogs get confused and eat them, and you see the poor things shaking," he added.

His words helped Julio understand the feeling he'd had since leaving Humahuaca: the impression that the changing landscape imitated the turns of Aliza's manuscript as it moved closer and closer to emptiness. It was the intuition, thought Julio, that everything in the story was slowly giving way to desert. The style was gradually shedding its baroque flourishes; the anecdotes, their excesses; the characters, the ties that kept them anchored in society. The village of the Nataibo was emptied of inhabitants, New Germany of dreams, and Aliza of words, in a sequence of images that crossed decades and continents but ended up carrying him towards that absolute emptiness he thought he was finding now, as the bus left the shakers behind and finally turned into the Salinas Grandes.

The perfectly white expanse stretched out in front of them, flaunting an imperial monotony. For the first time during his trip, Julio felt a little afraid, remembering that it was precisely the whiteness of the beast and not its size that had inspired terror in the sailors who hunted the great white whale in *Moby Dick*. Going further into the horizonless plain, he feared that Aliza had given him his own white whale, a fixed point that hid the incandescence of a senseless passion.

"Stopping!" he heard the driver shout in a shrill voice that shook him from his reflections.

Outside, about a hundred metres away, a saltpetre plant broke the monotony of the landscape. Letting his curiosity lead him, he decided to get off the bus there, knowing it wasn't the right stop and that later he would have to figure out how to reach Sarapura's town. It was only eight in the morning. He would have time to come up with a solution. Hiding among a group of tourists who were getting off another bus, he slipped in among the crowd that was taking a tour of what he would have thought was an abandoned station.

"The extraction period ends in November to avoid the rainy season," he heard the guide saying. "That's why everything is so quiet."

More than a plant it looked like a small ghost town. He remembered those small US mining towns relegated to oblivion by industry, ambition and history, and he was startled by their similarity to this still-functioning plant. A small cabin to shelter from the cold, an improvised stone church, and a pile of rusty machinery interrupted the landscape. Further on, he saw a series of perfectly symmetrical rectangular pools that made him think of the land artists' geological sculptures.

"The saltpetre is extracted from those pools," the guide said, before launching into an explanation of the complex process of salt production.

From all the details he heard, he was left only with the impression of a long process in which workers risked even their sight, besieged by the powerful sun that beat down on the plain.

"They call it 'surumpio' when the eyes give out," added the guide.

That mention of "surumpio" or "salinas sickness" made him think of the paradoxical similarity between the crystallisation process and the production of photographic negatives. He vaguely recalled something his father had mentioned about the origins of photography, an anecdote about the central role of salt in William Fox Talbot's invention. He seemed to remember that those first images were obtained through a technique called a salt print, and that memory, diverging from the blindness caused by the sun in the salinas, ended up returning him to the picture of Aliza that Olivia Walesi enclosed in the letter inviting him to Humahuaca. He liked to remember how it had all seemed like a possible scene from one of her novels, and to think how, if it were, someone surely would have mentioned the connection between salt and photography. He laughed to think that his reading of Aliza's manuscript, or maybe the repetition of her routine, had accidentally brought him closer to his friend's world. He imagined her walking though the white desert with Clarke and Sarapura, feeling that little by little words were evaporating, paradoxically paving the way for the book she had struggled for more than three decades to write. Writing conceived of as a kind of natural sculpture, carved out by patience and destiny, Julio thought as he watched a couple of locals setting up a souvenir stall by the roadside. Llamas carved into virgin salt, stones chiselled with archaeological shapes. Thinking of Aliza's manuscript, he told himself that precisely here was where Juvenal Suárez's courage lay: in his refusal to become a mere tourist object, one of thousands of pieces on display in that ever-expanding invisible museum that now, as the sun beat mercilessly down on the plain, was spreading out beyond the horizon and its mirages.

The day a group of doctors informed me of my aphasia, I didn't immediately think about Juvenal Suárez or von Mühlfeld. First I remembered the anecdote about that madman who, from his asylum in Broadmoor, contributed thousands of entries to the elaboration of the *Oxford English Dictionary*. I don't know why it was Dr William Minor's story that came to mind first. Victim of a trauma that dated back to the American Civil War, Minor had started to lose his grip on sanity. After a brief stint in a US asylum, he'd decided to move to London in an attempt to escape the fears that hounded him: at night, he swore he saw a crowd of men chasing him, trying to exact revenge for an old war crime. Years later, that paranoia would lead him to murder an innocent man and get him locked up for life in a British asylum, where, calm and surrounded by books, he would become one of the key protagonists in that titanic endeavour. I don't know why, but while the doctors were trying to explain what my illness would mean, I thought about William Minor, and something in me, conflicted but optimistic, said that only someone who has lost the immediacy and transparency of language is capable of finally seeing it in all its opacity: stubborn, exact, and hard as a rock. I also thought about the last days of Lenin, the great orator, mute and paralysed at the end of his life, unwittingly imitating the speechless final years of Émile Benveniste, the maestro of linguistics. I thought of children, of childhoods full of magical noise, and how we're incapable as adults of returning to that paradise of freewheeling sound. Convinced that every loss hides a gain, I remembered the story of Juvenal Suárez's dictionary, that serpentine adventure tale I'd struggled for more than a decade to tell.

For the first time in years, I opened my father's diaries. Those diaries that for a long time I had rejected with the same blind passion with which I'd once rejected my language, convinced that freedom began with the casting off of all past and all inheritance. In those first weeks, I limited myself to reading scattered fragments, as I felt how an awareness of the girl I'd once been returned to me, now clenched into a fist: the long evenings in Hampstead, my mother's elusive image, the smells of the garage where my father stored the tape recorder once he realised that taking up von Mühlfeld's project would be impossible. I went back over that inventory of memories and felt nostalgic for those rainy summers and for that man who had written, thirty years in advance, two lines that now became prophetic, an omen of the illness that was stealing away my language bit by bit. I read the phrase:

"the theatre of a voice doing battle with history,
the silences of a language doing battle with oblivion."

And I knew the time had come for me to quietly return to von Mühlfeld's story. I didn't stop there. I kept turning the diaries' yellowed pages until I saw the photograph of the two of them, the anthropologist and Juvenal Suárez, in front of Elisabeth Förster-Nietzsche's decrepit piano. A picture that shows them as what they were: an odd couple, united by solitude, eccentricity and obsession. I told myself that the tetralogy's last novel would begin there: by relating the singularity of an image that condenses the sad adventure I have tried to relate in these pages. A tale that closes in a loop and ends with me confronting the gaze of that man in whom my father had placed all his hopes, knowing all the while that his pursuit was doomed to fail. Juvenal Suárez, I realised, was my exact opposite. While he had more than enough words but lacked the world they described, the words of a still extant world were starting to fail me. It was then that I imagined the writing of this novel as a simple excuse to go deeper into the only project I cared about: writing that dictionary where I'd bury, as a secret or a private language, the truth behind my melancholy.

When language fails, quotations will remain:

"I catch myself ever more frequently repeating inane phrases, bits of half-forgotten conversations, absurd phrases derived from commonplaces that have stayed in my memory, or from songs I vaguely remember, or words my sister and I invented as children and that combined the languages we knew and others of which we barely had an idea, or quotations learned by heart (...) and all this in a series that I repeat when I'm alone as though to talk to myself, and that I wouldn't want anyone to overhear, since they would think I'm losing my mind (...). I also think about my friend who has lost her memory and who emits, sometimes, in a very hoarse voice because it's as though she's forgotten how to speak, absurd words that depend only on rhyme, cuchi cuchi, things like that (...). I wonder what the language of my senility will be."

Sylvia Molloy, *To Live between Languages*

From the sofa where he was sitting, Julio could see words carved into the mountain: "Welcome to San Antonio de los Cobres."

The taxi driver who brought him to the mining town had related some of the place's history: the predominance of copper in the mountain range that surrounded him, the dangerous levels of arsenic, the "train to the clouds" that connected the Argentine heights with the Chilean peaks, crossing the Andes at an altitude of more than four thousand metres. Julio imagined a train through the sky and imagined it would be like those moments of absolute weightlessness that come after a plane takes off, when it reaches the height of the clouds and dares to rise above them. Minutes later, when a right turn brought the mountains into view and he caught sight of the famous train's tracks, he was surprised to see that the clouds looked heavier and darker than he had imagined. At the foot of the mountain, he'd seen the shapes of the town where he now was. A hundred or so identical houses dotted the desert landscape, creating a serial effect that reminded him of the saltpetre pools. Beyond their monotony he could distinguish a big, green-roofed building that, he suspected, belonged to the same mining company that had erected the houses so precisely.

A handful of kids were running fearlessly through the streets, while the old folks peered warily at him from the pavements.

"Do you know where I can find Raúl Sarapura?" he asked two men who were sitting outside a general store.

"Parallel street that way, number 34," one of them said.

Moments later, knocking at the door of the house, he felt like the sound broke the atmosphere of lethargy that hung over the town. The third time he knocked, just when he was starting to think he'd got the wrong house, a dark-skinned man appeared sporting an imposing black moustache and a blue cap with the logo of a foreign company. He flung the door wide open as if he knew Julio and had been expecting him. Worried he was interrupting and convinced that the man was in a rush to go somewhere, Julio started to introduce himself, but was surprised to hear an invitation to come in. He'd barely stammered out his name before Sarapura disappeared down the hall of the small house, then returned with two full mate gourds and a cigarette between his lips.

And that was precisely the sense that came over him again now as his host picked up his story: the intuition that this man had been patiently awaiting his arrival.

"So you knew Alicia way back when," he heard Sarapura say in a hoarse, deliberate voice.

Julio turned his gaze from the window back to his interlocutor, not without first pausing on the photograph he'd recognised minutes earlier: a portrait of Sarapura next to Aliza and the greyhound on the salt flats. He'd noticed it as soon as he entered the house, but hadn't mentioned it. He was surprised by the man's naturalness as he ushered Julio in and offered him a seat, then handed him the mate he was now sipping. Minutes later, more relaxed, Julio allowed himself to look around, and his gaze lit again on the portrait. But more than the photo itself, it was a small drawing beside it that had caught his attention.

According to Saussure, this double river is the image of thought and language.

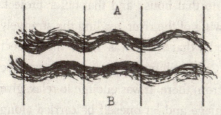

The trick, then, would be to learn to pass from one bank to the other without ceasing to speak.

"The trick, then, would be to learn to pass from one bank of the river to the other without ceasing to speak." The suggestion, a bit ludicrous and a bit funny, that Aliza's whole project could be reduced to a bizarre diving exercise made him smile. At the margins of the most tragic tonalities of that story were Juvenal Suárez's laughter, mentions of Jules Verne's adventures, and childhood games. An underground story, written against the grain, the meaning of which was crystallised in the smiles of Raúl Sarapura and Aliza Abravanel posing for the camera in the picture of them on the salt flats, like a weightless and friendly version of that photo of Juvenal Suárez and Karl-Heinz von Mühlfeld posing in front of Elisabeth Förster-Nietzsche's piano. It was a feeling of lightness that took on resonance against the background of Sarapura's tone, everyday and objective – some might say disinterested – as he narrated the chronology and details of the elaboration of what he called the *Dictionary*. It was as if it had been clear from the very beginning that the only significance of the manuscript of *A Private Language* was that it would guide him to that house and that other project. Looking again at the drawing of the river, reading the strangely lucid phrase, Julio thought that Aliza was right: the project depended on lightness. On distilling language to its essence and starting to rebuild it from there. It was enough to relax, give in to the current of language and let oneself be carried along by those same waters that had ultimately brought him to that small house in San Antonio de los Cobres.

"Yes, I knew her long before the books," Julio replied. "But you've also known her a long time, right?"

"Yes, since that first trip," said Sarapura, going on to explain.

In the eighties, his father had been Aliza's guide on her travels through the region, and perhaps that's why he'd been the one the writer contacted as soon as she decided to spend her final years in the desert. Raúl's father was working at the salinas in those years, so he decided to delegate Abravanel's request to his son. Thus began a relationship that over the years would turn into collaboration, but that at first consisted of the most mundane tasks. In those early days, before Walesi and Escobar came to Humahuaca, Sarapura helped her in the most basic jobs: buying food, making repairs to the house, taking her to town and back.

"I saw her laughing about the words that wouldn't come to her and I took an interest in her condition," he said. "I spent nights reading about different available treatments, memorising strategies that I'd use with her later."

In those days Aliza was struggling fruitlessly to start the final book of the tetralogy of ecological novels, which was to be titled *Strata* and correspond to the element of earth. More than once during that time he was witness to her frustration with that project, which seemed beyond her reach. Moved, he decided to take the matter of therapy seriously, convinced that Aliza could get better with his help.

"I don't remember where, but at some point I read about a linguistic therapy based on musical associations, and I remembered how when I first met her she mentioned she loved the piano, so I suggested we give it a try."

To his surprise, after balking at first, Aliza agreed. And so, for more than two years, they sat together at the town's piano, trying to use rhythm to rebuild the bridges that her illness was breaking down. Little could he know that his therapy would open the way to her future conception and construction of the *Dictionary*.

Shaken, Julio let him talk, and simultaneously went on taking in his surroundings. In spite of the house's minimalism, it held clear signs of the friendship between Sarapura and Abravanel. On some shelves near the kitchen, along with a stereo and a pile of old CDs, he saw books that he assumed had once belonged to Aliza. Old editions of Onetti, Woolf, Faulkner, Bernhard. During the moments when Sarapura excused himself and disappeared back into the kitchen to stir the soup he was cooking, Julio even made out, among the many books, a copy of the Spanish translation of *Under the Volcano.*

"Eventually, she started to include me in her attempts at writing," said Sarapura, lighting a cigarette.

At first, his contribution was minor: reminding her of some forgotten word or suggesting a synonym in the process of writing what would become *Strata.* Gradually, Aliza began to include him in everything, perhaps aware that her condition called for a sort of four-handed writing. On one of those afternoons, while he was reviewing the author's archive in search of a story she had asked for, he found a file on which was scrawled, as a tentative title: *Sketches for A Private Language/Dictionary of Loss.* Overcome by curiosity, he opened it, and as he started to read he was surprised to find what seemed to be a kind of allegory of the loss of language. Confused, convinced the writer was in no condition to have written those pages, he put them away.

"I was quiet that whole week, trying to understand what I'd read."

Ten days later, when he returned to the archive to nose around, this time in secret, he realised that those pages seemed to have been written before Abravanel had come to Humahuaca.

"Before her aphasia," he reiterated.

Impressed by her inexplicable premonition, he decided to take the pages home. That was where, after finishing the unusual tale, convinced it was autobiographical and true, he decided to mention his discovery to Aliza.

"At first she didn't want to tell me anything," explained Sarapura.

"And how did you convince her?" Asked Julio.

"Little by little, with patience."

In those first weeks, Abravanel refused to recognise herself in those pages. The therapy continued, as did her attempts to keep writing *Strata*, until it became clear that the project exceeded the limits imposed by her condition. That was when, perhaps reconsidering her situation, the author decided to go back to her old draft. It must have been during those months when Aliza started to imagine the end goal that would ultimately occupy her and Sarapura. In those windy, dry months of the cold desert winter, she realise that what her work needed, more than a final push, was a new strategy. And so she surrendered to the project on which she would spend her final days.

"The dictionary that's already cost you a trip here, and that will also get you stuck in a downpour if I don't hurry with the *locro*," said Sarapura.

Julio watched him walk towards the kitchen, then looked out of the window. Sarapura was right: the passing hours had darkened the sky. In the distance, the tracks of the Train to the Clouds seemed to disappear in the darkness, like a tightrope awaiting an aerialist. It was time to go, he thought, as he watched Sarapura return with two bowls of soup and what looked like a book under his arm. He realised it was too late to excuse himself as he watched his interlocutor set down an old notebook where he read the words: *Dictionary of Loss*. Like this, the manuscript looked simple, almost vulgar: the rudimentary project of a primary school child. Few would have imagined it was the culmination of the complex and baroque pages he had started reading days before. Without much explanation, Sarapura opened the notebook, and from its pages fell a single sheet on which was written: "For Julio Gamboa, who will know how to find the path that leads to these pages." Julio was surprised to find that the calligraphy was different, rounder and calmer than the strokes that used to characterise Aliza's handwriting. What he heard next dispelled his doubts. As he sipped the *locro*, Sarapura told him how, once the choral writing of the project was conceived, he'd set out to study Abravanel's work in an attempt to make sure the manuscript maintained stylistic unity.

"Something like a piano arrangement for four hands," he explained.

He'd spent a couple of years trying to find himself in Abravanel's voice, copying from memory and then erasing extensive passages of the manuscript, until one day, sitting in a bar, he thought he'd understood the motivation of that voice that would accompany him in the elaboration of the text Julio now held in his hands. Afraid of finding himself in the notebook, Julio chose to stick with the intuition that told him it was time to take his leave. He would have time to peruse the notebook in the coming days.

"I'm sorry to leave so abruptly," said Julio. "But I'll have to cross the salinas in the rain."

"You're right, the summer rains stop for no-one," said Sarapura, slapping him on the back.

Saying his goodbyes, Julio thought it was strange that Sarapura's name didn't appear on the cover of the notebook and that he didn't ask to be acknowledged in the slightest. He imagined the man some months later, back at work on those eye-watering, back-breaking salt flats. Outside, he looked back at the photo of Sarapura with Aliza, both of them smiling against the white expanse. Looking at the dark clouds over the mountains, he smiled to think that Aliza was right: the trick lay in learning to move from one bank to the other without ceasing to speak. With the downpour imminent, he took his leave and was preparing to walk to the station when he made out a taxi in the distance.

5

On the trip back to Humahuaca, Julio remembered a simple phrase that Sarapura had offered as a kind of conjecture: "Only someone who knows he is condemned can clearly see the path to salvation." Absorbed as he was in the tale of the dictionary's making, he'd let the comment pass. Now, sitting in the taxi as it made its way through the downpour, he re-evaluated the words. Sarapura was right. The phrase made him think of Kafka, imagining parables of impossible salvation while all around him, still silent, the future Nazi forces grew. He thought of Proust, asthmatic in bed while he breathed life into his sentences. He thought of Nietzsche himself, signing his diatribes from the margins of madness. He thought, finally, of Aliza, for whom fate and illness had decided that only right at the end would she find the lens through which to understand her family history. He particularly remembered the final pages of *A Private Language*, in which Aliza, perhaps aware that her own voice was fading, decided to lean on other voices. Quotations arranged collage-like among the pages, as if they were ruins hinting at the outlines of a still unrecognisable mosaic.

He had seen something similar in the pages of the dictionary Sarapura had just shown him: a cocktail of photographs, found objects, definitions and short fragments that reminded him of the haikus his grandfather had made him memorise as a kid. Unlike with those childish pages that he'd approached with innocence and joy, something made him put this newly found notebook aside. Looking out at the grey blanket spread over the salt flats, Julio remembered the work in progress with which Walesi and Escobar were trying to pay homage to Aliza's memory: that map traced in white chalk on the dry desert plains, lines the rain must be currently dissolving. At first he felt sorry for the artists. So many months of work only to watch as nature swallowed the piece. On second thoughts, he decided it was the perfect culmination. Nature retaking its place in the labyrinths of culture, gradually moving further down its corridors and imposing its will.

It was still raining when they reached Humahuaca. The town, stripped of the local craftsmen who usually dotted the landscape, seemed sadder and lonelier now. Suddenly loquacious, the taxi driver pointed at a school and started talking about the multiple trips Eva Perón had made to the region in the early fifties, to which a dozen half-empty school buildings testified. Julio let him talk, happy to be returning after a long day. He remembered how that same morning he'd thought he'd seen a fixed point flashing in the night, and how that illusion had made him set off in search of Sarapura. Now he was returning, dictionary in hand, with the feeling of having discovered the enigma behind Aliza's manuscript. He saw the commune's houses rise up through the curtain of rain and prepared to relate his findings to Olivia Walesi, but he was surprised to find Clarke sprawled on the floor and the house in absolute silence. Relieved, he dropped the dictionary on the desk and flopped on the bed, and the dog jumped up to join him. When he heard the door open some minutes later, he pretended to be asleep. There would be time to decipher his trip to the Salinas Grandes.

Later, only the laughter would remain. The echo of a laugh that at first he thought was a sob, then a howl or a sigh, but recognised as what it really was when he finally dared to leave the table with the half-finished chess game and move further down the corridor, chasing the reverberation of that anarchic whisper, and came to a half-open door. He peered in and saw the scene he would later relate in his diary: the room perfectly white except for a desk clock, and beside it the nurse trying to calm the anthropologist, while his eyes, unrecognisable, looked laughingly at the tangle of tape he had strung around the room like a giant, childish spiderweb. That muddle of now-useless tape that my father recognised as the end of the story this man had spent the past five days telling him. A story to which he had briefly considered himself heir and that was now ending abruptly, to the rhythm of the nurse's soothing ministrations, while beside her, leaning against the door, another, younger nurse with reddish hair watched the scene, and, perhaps out of nervousness, immaturity, or mere contagion, started laughing too.

Enough to say:

"A writer is an odd thing. He's a contradiction, and he makes no sense. Writing also means not speaking. Keeping silent. Screaming without sound. A writer is often quite restful; she listens a lot. She doesn't speak much because it's impossible to speak to someone about a book one has written, and especially about a book one is writing."

Marguerite Duras, *Writing*

To write is, sometimes, to speak in silence.

Sitting on the plane that would return him to Buenos Aires, Julio first felt the pull of gravity on take-off, followed by that graceful moment when the plane reaches the sky and levels off, and everything turns light and weightless like the clouds themselves. Only then did he allow his thoughts to turn to Raúl Sarapura. He imagined him in a moment of tedium, sitting in a rocking chair and drinking mate, staring off towards the mountains where from time to time he saw the famous train emerge. He guessed the man would be more relaxed now, aware that Aliza Abravanel's secret was far away, and his function as guardian was coming to an end. Feeling the weight of his newly inherited responsibility, Julio opened his backpack. He dug through his socks and shirts until he found, among the disarray of things that had accompanied him over recent days, the place where he'd carefully stowed the two manuscripts he now had to bear.

PART TWO

Dictionary of Loss

You used to read dictionaries like other people read novels. Every entry is a character, you'd say, who might be encountered on some other page. Plots, many of them, would form during any random reading. The story changes according to the order in which the entries are read. A dictionary resembles the world more than a novel does, because the world is not a coherent sequence of actions, but a constellation of things perceived.

Édouard Levé, *Suicide*

PART TWO

Dictionary of Loss

I

The early morning was both island and refuge. The fox had disappeared, leaving the street in the inclement care of the storm. Julio watched it go before turning back towards the face on the screen. In half light, as if the photograph had been taken at dusk, the tired eyes of a copper-skinned man offered the hope of a destination. He thought he could distinguish, in that evasive gaze, the direction he had pursued fruitlessly over recent days. Below the photo it said: *Juan de Paz Raymundo in his Theatre of Memory, Amajchel, Guatemala.* He recognised the place with the gladness of one connecting clues, but instead of immediately looking for his discovery on a map, he returned to that face: not timid, but something in it seemed to be withdrawing. Through the window, wrapped in a white shroud, the early morning imitated that double gesture of surrender and concealment.

Many times over the course of the years, this sofa had acted as his refuge. On more than a few nights of insomnia he had come to lie there, facing a picture window that framed a view of the street he knew so well. A certain calm and peace flooded the house at those early hours, a certain clarity effectively buried later on by the activity of the day. He'd kiss Marie-Hélène without waking her, take a book and lie on that sofa where he'd learned to look at the dawn with an owl's eyes, attentive to those minimal scenes that hide behind the monotony of the night in the dark: occasional shouts from drunk students, the to and fro of nocturnal animals, silhouettes of other backlit insomniacs. Trivial stories in search of a patient and attentive witness. He would sit there in the light of a small lamp and surrender to his reading, until he felt that the book's universe slowly blended with the world outside the window.

Usually, the sound of his wife calling him would invite him back to their room. Today, however, it had been the memory of her voice that had woken him up completely.

"Amajchel," he thought he'd heard her say.

Uselessly, he turned his body towards her, but the cold folds of the sheets confirmed what he already knew: his wife was far away, and that word had been only an echo of the pages he had read that afternoon. Since his return the entire house had become an echo chamber, and within its walls, Marie-Hélène's voice played at melding with Aliza's. He didn't evoke them, but the voices came to him, half-formed phrases and expressions, building this furtive dialogue that he now felt was infiltrating even his dreams.

Unable to sleep, he had taken Aliza's manuscripts and gone to sit on the sofa. Outside, the snowstorm that had begun in the early afternoon was threatening to obscure the view. Covered in white, the street recalled the desert salt flats he had recently left. Apart from the wind that shook the treetops, little moved outside. Even so, his well-trained eye had distinguished the shape of a solitary fox that faced the storm without fear. He recognised it immediately: it had appeared out of nowhere when he'd returned from Humahuaca, usually accompanied by two smaller foxes. He often saw them in the afternoon, prowling around his neighbour's garden, looking for food in the rubbish bins or taking shelter from the rain under the garage roof.

"You behave like a dog," Marie-Hélène had told him.

The memory of that sentence in the empty house accentuated the differences between those foxes and the trembling little dog that had looked at him from the crate. Maybe the trick lay in learning to go from domesticity to nomadism. Today, the two smaller foxes had melted away, leaving their leader alone in the elements, isolated and exposed like a tenacious Arctic explorer. Accompanied by that animal in whose wanderings he would like to recognise himself, he had returned to his reading. He would read a few entries and then get distracted, looking out of the window again. He followed the fox's trajectory, the progress of the storm, and the gradual disappearance of the sleighs and Santa Clauses that were already heading towards disuse.

Now, however, the fox had vanished again. Through the blizzard, Julio looked for it where he had spotted it before: it wasn't on the neighbour's steps, or in the garage, or beside the cars. In the utterly deserted landscape, the storm reigned. The snow had swallowed the night, opening the way to the revelation he thought he'd just had. Unable to share the discovery with anyone, he turned back to the screen. There they were: the jet-black eyes still confronting him from the distance, wrapped in an aura of clarity that reminded him of Aliza. *Juan de Paz Raymundo in his Theatre of Memory, Amajchel, Guatemala,* he read again below the photo. He picked up the *Dictionary of Loss* and turned to the letter M. There he read: "Yes: I am the mute woman who lives in Giulio Camillo's theatre of memory." A little further down he found the line he was looking for: "I remember the mute gaze of Juan de Paz Raymundo." The week before, he'd read the phrase dozens of times, but only now did he understand its importance.

ALICIA ABRAVANEL

DICTIONARY OF LOSS

2

It hadn't been easy to get there. At first the path that led from *A Private Language* to *Dictionary of Loss* seemed just as distant, intricate and remote as the one that would have led from Humahuaca to Amajchel. He returned to Cincinnati on Christmas Eve, only to find the house empty and the tree dry and yellowed. He had forgotten to throw it out, though Marie-Hélène had asked him to, as if deep down he'd harboured a wish to find her there too on his return.

"Coming home to family?" the taxi driver had asked him.

And he, ashamed, nodded in silence. Through the window he saw the rusted silhouettes of Gary Works, the steel mill whose billowing steam and tall stacks made him think of San Antonio de los Cobres and Raúl Sarapura. Then the industrial landscape gave way to the suburbs he knew so well, and he felt he'd left Humahuaca far behind, with its artist communes and open-air parties. The Christmas tree, dry but perfectly decorated, was his only welcome.

In an attempt to distract himself, he started spending several hours a day at the office. He left the house early, just before sunrise. He liked to coincide with the dawn as he arrived at the campus emptied of students and full of snow. He would reach his office, put the coffee on, and spend the next hours randomly reading pages of the manuscript of *A Private Language* and looking for information about the Nataibo and von Mühlfeld, about Abravanel and Juvenal Suárez. When he tired of that, he took out the dictionary and put it on the table. He found its simple cover endearing, almost like a school notebook, on which Aliza had written her name above a drawing of the coloured peaks he had just left behind. He opened it and skimmed the collage of images that wound sinuously around the entries: old index cards with typewritten words; childish drawings and postcards; archival documents that referred to the world of mineral ecology; old photographs, torn and stained, in which Julio looked for her without success. Unhurriedly, he surrendered to the pleasure of recognising images from the stories he'd recently read, with all the spontaneity of one who remembers book covers better than their plots. At five in the afternoon he locked up the office and walked back home, aware that when he opened the door, the remains of his fight with Marie-Hélène would confront him: the broken flowerpot, soil strewn over the tiles, the half-packed suitcase. Refusing to clean it up was his way of accepting that the problem was still there, even if everything seemed to be in order.

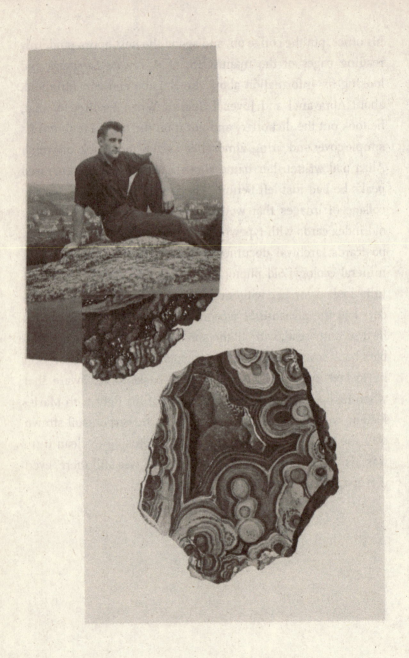

In those first readings, one image in particular had caught his attention: a black and white portrait showing a dapper man posing on a rock, with a handful of houses that could just be glimpsed in the distance. The man in the photo reminded him of Elvis. This reference, which set the picture in the seventies, suggested it was Aliza's father posing there. A second correlation convinced him he was right. Superimposed over the image was the transverse cut of a rock whose interior had been digitally retouched to emphasize the geometry of the mineral forms. A visual game that was repeated some pages further on, this time disrupting a portrait of the Austrian philosopher Ludwig Wittgenstein.

In mid afternoon, Julio had recognised that countenance with nostalgia. He remembered it had been Aliza who had first talked to him about that eccentric thinker, as they drove towards Guatemala.

"I think Wittgenstein is fascinating, even though he reminds me of my father."

He could see her now, stretched out in the Cherokee's back seat, reading a novel by Thomas Bernhard in which she said she detected the philosopher's influences. He recalled how, during their trip, her retelling of the Austrian's life had coincided with the landscape of war they saw out of the window.

Of that now-remote time when the reading of *Correction* had led them to the philosopher's eccentricities, he remembered their astonishment at the mystical turns his thinking would take when it came into contact with the catastrophes of the First World War. Aliza was particularly captivated by the decision Wittgenstein had made in mid 1914, believing that only direct confrontation with death would be capable of producing the meaning in his life that he'd been fruitlessly seeking in academia. That decision to leave everything behind and enlist in the Austro-Hungarian army awoke the utmost admiration in her, convinced as she was that those events illustrated the dramatic thesis that so seduced her in those days: the idea that thought could find clarity only by confronting the abyss.

It was 1982. Only five years earlier, the poet Roque Dalton had been cut down in El Salvador, and the memory of the deceased Sandinista leader Carlos Fonseca Amador still flew low over Central American thinking. It was no surprise that Aliza – the young punk who had come to Nicaragua seeking to escape her parents' suffocating presence, a young photo-journalist who, like Wittgenstein himself, had traded in the halls of Cambridge for precarious battlefields – felt she'd found a kind of light-house in the philosopher's daring decision.

"Just think, he finished writing the *Tractatus* in a POW camp," she'd said.

Julio thought he understood why it had been Wittgenstein and not Dalton who'd won their early devotion. He sensed that what fascinated them about the Austrian was the courage it took to make that wager on thought, even in wartime. A courage that had little to do with the "committed literature" of the time, and that was depicted in the mystical tonalities his ideas took on in those years. That step by which mathematical logic opened up towards a deeper meditation, able to gesture towards the ineffable. A total gamble on the atemporality of art that Abravanel herself had evoked when she decided they would cross the region in the midst of the armed conflict. When he looked at it like that, the idea seemed clear and beautiful: not so much taking the war to thought or thought to war, but rather learning to inhabit the brief peace that cracks opens between the two when they meet face to face.

That association between the images of Aliza's father and Wittgenstein had been the bridge that led the entries in the text not only to begin to make sense, but also to conjure up the memory of his old friend. For the first time, Julio intuited his own place in it all, and the dark logic that marked the movement from one manuscript to the other. Since his return to Cincinnati, he'd felt impotent before the dictionary: too many possible points of entry, too many coded trajectories. Now, finally, he thought he saw a possible path.

Earlier that day, consulting the philosopher's biography, he found the detail that finally convinced him he was on the right track. He read how Wittgenstein, after returning to Cambridge on the eve of the Second World War, had concentrated his efforts on a central subject: the impossibility of a private language. The coincidence with the title of Aliza's posthumous manuscript ultimately awoke another memory. He remembered how on the way to Honduras, Aliza had tried to explain the concept to him herself.

"Imagine that when you're born, you're given a box with a beetle inside. You're told that it's so valuable and personal that no-one but you can see it."

"Now that's a strange world," he said with a laugh.

Then she had gone on to explain how, in the philosopher's thought experiment, the whole world went around delighting in their own personal beetles, never having seen anyone else's, only their own.

"Now, what are they referring to, in that hypothetical world, every time they use the word beetle?" she asked.

To that question, Wittgenstein replied: to the social act of imagining it, never to the beetle itself, which could very well not exist. Julio had liked the experiment in spite of its twisted logic, or maybe precisely because of it. Looking out at the campus lawn covered in snow, he again imagined that Kafkaesque universe where everyone walks around carrying their beetle in a box, everyone paranoid and imagining the differences between the boxes' contents, unable to know if they are talking about the same thing, or if some hidden god is doubled over laughing at his own joke. Wittgenstein, however, had not imagined this in a comic key. The Austrian had understood that merely swapping the name of the enigmatic beetle for the word "pain" would emphasise the importance of that dark parable.

That memory made him return to the photograph in which the philosopher's face appeared cut in half, his mouth turned to stone. Under that portrait was a quote: "Another person cannot have my pains. *My* pains – what are they?" The possibility of language played out on that border between two beings trying to talk about their sorrows. Before him, vast, deep, painful, the gaze of the man who had uttered those words looked like proof of their truth. Julio tried to shake off this feeling of fearful clairvoyance, remembering his recent laughter at a world full of beetles, but then the memory of his friend rose up again. He flipped ahead in the pages until he reached the entry dedicated to the word *Private*. On the old card, under the Greek etymology of the word, she had written: "I think of Juvenal Suárez, I think of myself: poor idiots, the Greeks would say."

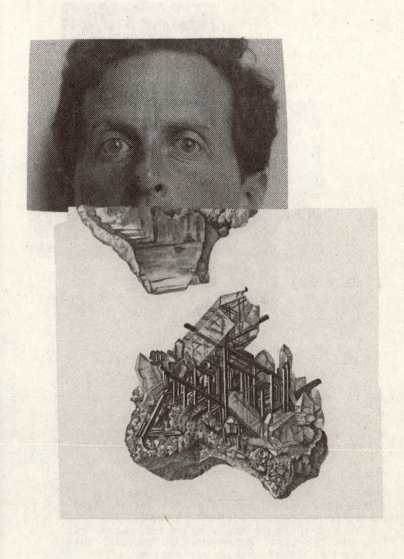

panorama;
pronounce;
privation;

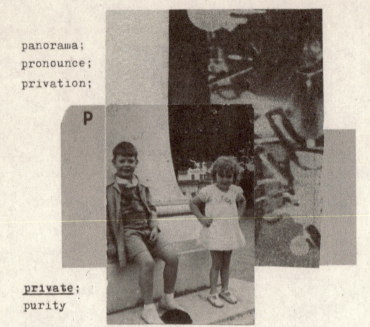

<u>private</u>;
purity

In Latin, the word "idiot" comes from the
ancient Greek, ἰδιώτης meaning "a private
citizen; individual." In ancient Athens,
it was used to refer to a person who decides
to separate himself from public life.

I think of Juvenal Suárez, I think of
myself: poor idiots, the Greeks would say.

—

While I was taking pictures of that game
of marbles or "cincos", one of the children
noticed my camera pointed at them. He
walked over to me and started telling me off
in his language. I answered in Spanish, but
I soon realised it was useless: an abyss
yawned between my language and his. That
was a dialogue between two idiots condemned
not to understand one another.

3

Now, well into the small hours, Julio thought he recognised in the face displayed on the screen the same keen, tormented gaze he'd seen in Wittgenstein. The same tired eyes in which he could sense the passion of a person who has dedicated their life to chasing an idea to its logical conclusions. Further down, the news article described the idea specific to this case, hinting at the obsession that had led Juan de Paz Raymundo to leave the city behind and go deep into the forgotten territory of Amajchel.

At first when he'd opened the article, Julio thought it was a literary profile. Instead what he found was a news story about the atrocities committed during the Guatemalan genocide in the eighties. The text went on to describe how Raymundo had built, in one of the towns that had been razed by military forces, an enormous open-air theatre that, he theorised, would help survivors recover the memories they had buried after living through trauma. He said his project was modelled on the works of the renaissance philosopher Giulio Camillo, whose posthumous work *L'Idea del theatro* drew on both Greek mnemonic studies and Medieval hermetic sciences in its attempt to imagine a theory of knowledge that was also a staging of memory. Following those schematics, he had designed his own theatre of memory, through which he sought to take the pain out of forgetting.

A gust of wind shook the windows, interrupting his reading and prompting him to look around. The house seemed to be dozing, ignoring the storm, submerged in an absolute stillness, and it was on nights like this that he felt Marie-Hélène's absence was becoming more conspicuous than ever. It had been her voice that woke him up at dawn, giving him the key that had led him to this discovery. But she wasn't there. Sometimes she called in the mornings, just to keep Julio from feeling too lonely. She told him anecdotes about her family and explained how, unlike him, she had come to accept that she had been Americanised by so many years away from France.

"My parents almost killed me when I said that."

He listened to her and laughed, but couldn't help feeling that something in her voice was pulling further away. On the nights when he was unable to find the manuscripts' meaning and felt he had come to a dead end, he would often go to the room that served as Marie-Hélène's architecture studio. He used to like to look at the scale models, those worlds in miniature that opened up onto hypothetical futures. Lately, though, in her absence, those models had taken on the same spectral character that now, in the midst of the storm, threatened to take over the house.

A theatre of memory, Julio repeated aloud. He tried to imagine Juan de Paz Raymundo immersed in the construction of that delirious project, but the image of Aliza distracted him again.

Perhaps that was her secret intention: to force him to conjure up the past that he himself, without knowing exactly why, had tried to erase. He turned the pages of the dictionary until he came to the photograph of Wittgenstein. Then he understood his mistake: it wasn't exhaustion that those eyes communicated, but rather the strange lucidity of the insomniac. He looked back at Juan de Paz Raymundo. There he was, admonishing him from that other shore towards which he felt he was heading.

language, lament, **lucidity** , locale

To misplace language. Lose the common
place.
        Explore the elements
        stripped of flags.

Lucidity: to be in the open pampa and
watch the rabbit as it escapes.
        To start to talk once the commonplace
        cliché has fallen.

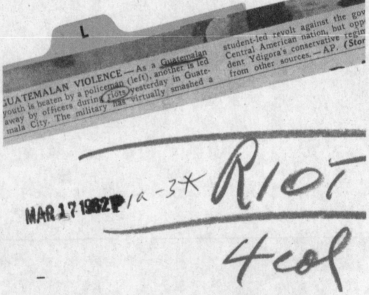

GUATEMALAN VIOLENCE — As a Guatemalan
youth is beaten by a policeman (left), another is led
away by officers during riots yesterday in Guatemala City. The military has virtually smashed a
student-led revolt against the gov
Central American nation, but opp
dent Ydigora's conservative regim
from other sources. — AP. (Stor

RIOT

MAR 17 1962 P/a-3*

4col

Of that town I remember the smiles of the
children and their eyes fixed on the ground.
A white circle defined the space of play,
and nothing outside it mattered.
Blank slate, razed earth:the marbles
battling among the ruins.
And the sense that no photograph would
do it justice.

4

The game of echoes between Aliza's father and Wittgenstein had opened up the path that had been blocked until then. He grasped that the *Dictionary of Loss* was nothing but the mirror image of *A Private Language*. On more than one occasion he had sensed that the dictionary was composed of a series of inversions. The photographs appeared twice, first showing the front and then the back, and that usually invisible facet was where the keys to interpretation were often to be found. Unconsciously, he'd let that theory of the reverse guide his reading of the philosopher's life as an entrance into the father's, and now it grew into a generalised intuition: if he could understand the meaning of the image he saw there, he would understand his own life as the photographic negative of Aliza's.

The memory of his friend laughing as she talked about Wittgenstein's beetles gave him the other key. He suspected that he should follow the routes drawn by that laugh. The roads that, within the text, guided him along winding Central American streets. "Does writing *your* name here turn this into a letter?" she had written on one of the last pages. At first he'd been surprised to find that question there without an apparent interlocutor. He thought it could be her father, but the echoes of memory convinced him that he was the addressee. Aliza Abravanel had imagined those pages as a letter in which she reproached him for something. And she'd sent that letter from Guatemala. Amajchel was the other side of Humahuaca.

Zeno

Zeno of Elea, a Greek philosopher who lived five centuries before Christ, spent many hours thinking about the possibility of movement. His is the famous paradox about Achilles and the tortoise, in which the Greek warrior is unable to catch up with the tortoise, no matter how close he gets.

In Zeno's world, you could get infinitely close to the other, but never right beside him.

—

At the end of the journey, immense distance.

That evening, the snow forced him to stay late at the office. Encouraged, he returned to his reading from his new-found angle. He thought he understood that his indirect approach to the dictionary was nothing more than a digression to avoid the guilt he felt towards it. He set aside the more enigmatic fragments and started reading the narrative centred on Guatemala. He could sense a traumatic scene that Aliza had never been able to forget. Julio hadn't been there, precisely because he hadn't dared follow her to the end, where everything led to a simple but piercing scene of a group of children playing marbles in the ruins of a town reduced to razed earth. "And what do *you* know?", her voice rebuked him from the final pages, and he recognised himself in that *you*, ignorant and useless, incapable of crossing the border that separated his own pain from others'. He remembered the beetles and told himself that the Austrian was right, and language only worked if someone dared to cross that border. The image of Aliza doing battle with her aphasia, trying to tell a final story from the distant lands of Humahuaca, corrected his intuition: literature was precisely what arose when language foundered. The *Dictionary* was Aliza's final effort, a letter reproaching him for his lack of courage and delegating to him those fragments like ruins from which to reconstruct lost experience. Julio paused his reading and looked up. Outside, the snow had stopped falling and now spread out like a blanket of oblivion.

Lacking speech. the infant plays.
His game imitates society to scale.
I remember how when I was a child
my father always told me:
"Careful with your games"
As if he knew that games also
have consequences.

—

On April 15, 1982, I arrived in the area
of Amajchel and found a village in ruins.
And amid those ruins, as if nothing or
very little had happened, I saw five K'iché
children playing marbles.
"Cincos," they called them.
"Butchers," the game was called.
I sensed that in the game, in the subtle
violence of its name, they were imitating
something sinister.
Take pictures, I'd been told.

So I did.

He walked home, following the scant light from the street lamps. His footsteps, sinking into the still intact snow, lent him serenity, helping him organise his multiple impressions. *Folderol*, he remembered Aliza writing as an echolalia in the dictionary, and for a second he wanted language and memory to be like that too: lightning flashes of meaning, able to express in one stroke the totality of a world. Snowfall, overall, wherewithal: the world reduced to basic expression. He remembered that in his reading, one date in particular – that fateful April 10, 1982 when the writer had crossed the border between El Salvador and Guatemala – emerged as the black hole around which this universe of scattered pieces gathered. A date that summarised the text and made him think back to the road trip they had started on together in early spring. As he walked home, he tried again to conjure up the details of the trip.

He remembered afternoons of anxiety and expectation leading up to it, his mother's complaints and the hum of his father's Cherokee Jeep every time it started up. He saw himself in the thermal springs southeast of Liberia, en route to Nicaragua, and then drinking beers in Managua with a group of Aliza's Sandinista friends, before heading northwards where the Momotombo volcano seemed to have been awaiting them for ages. He called up the memory of an afternoon in Honduras on the banks of the Nacaome River, and then another one of the impressive Cerro Las Minas. He saw Aliza at the wheel on the Salvadoran streets during what must have been the final days of March 1982 or the beginning of April, when the presence of war in those lands was becoming apparent. He even salvaged the image of a border full of soldiers. The memory made him feel all over again the anxiety that had stayed with him during the final days of the trip, much as Aliza tried to calm him by reading Roque Dalton poems aloud, like someone challenging the gods by shouting blasphemy. He saw himself, young, nervous and northbound, getting dangerously close to that date when he would finally part ways with Aliza.

He couldn't remember much more. "I don't know what I saw that day," she had written in reference to the scene glimpsed in Amajchel, but the words could well serve to describe his own situation regarding the events of that April 10. He tried to remember the name of the town where he had left Aliza, but a sound distracted him. He was passing the library, and in a nearby field a family of deer was gazing at him intently. Though the scene had occurred many times over the years, it always held something of chimera and illusion, more so now that the snow seemed to be suspending time, emphasising the fragility of the moment. He tried to approach the deer slowly, but the noise of a nearby bicycle startled them, and he could only watch as they disappeared back into the woods.

memory,
river

———

laughter

According to Saussure, this double river
is the image of thought and language.

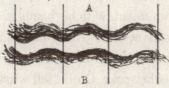

The trick, then, would be to learn to pass
from one bank to the other without
ceasing to speak.

I remember how at some point, the boy
stopped talking, and he pointed at me and
started to laugh. Then the other children
stopped playing and laughed along with him.

5

The echoes of that scene reverberated now that the storm was abating, leaving the street as orphaned and secretive as he had found it the night he'd seen the deer. Julio contemplated the limpid landscape and remembered the photo of Aliza beside Sarapura, smiling on the salt flats. "The trick, then, would be to learn to pass from one bank to the other without ceasing to speak," it said beneath the photo. In the early morning hours, the words made him smile as he returned to the article before him.

In this new article, Juan de Paz Raymundo was photographed in profile, captured mid movement. With his hands in the air and his eyes turned upwards, he seemed to be invoking the presence of someone who was gone, though most likely the photo had caught him unawares as he spoke. On his left wrist he wore a bracelet with colourful patterns that were repeated first by his open-collared shirt and then by the wool hat on top of his long, wavy black hair. His dark skin and narrow eyes were indigenous features, but Julio couldn't tell if they were K'iche' or Kaqchikel. Depicted like that, mid speech, his profile took on an air of mystery that only increased on a second look, when Julio noticed the countless objects surrounding the man: empty bottles, religious candles, newspapers, sculptures and a handful of old photos he tried unsuccessfully to decipher.

"It's about digging up the past," Juan de Paz had told the interviewer, trying to explain the logic of his theatre.

Looking at the image, Julio went back over the long chain of survivors he had followed to reach that man. He thought of Elisabeth Förster-Nietzsche and Bernhard Förster, lost amid the ruins of their own delirium. He thought of Karl-Heinz von Mühlfeld and Yitzhak Abravanel, trapped in attempts to save a history that wasn't theirs. He thought of Juvenal Suárez, ensconced in the old mansion in New Germany, arcane guardian of an entire culture. He thought of the play of echoes and legacies that propelled forward a story that was stubbornly anchored in the past. He thought of Aliza, writing those pages like someone writing a letter to the future, aware that she wouldn't be there to give testimony but trusting that her writing would find a way to resonate in a present where she no longer played a part.

"I am the mute who lives in Giulio Camillo's theatre of memory," she had written.

Julio tried to picture her there, among the collection of stuff that surrounded Juan de Paz Raymundo, but it was the memory of Marie-Hélène's face that emerged instead. At the end of the day, it had been her voice in his sleep that had finally directed him to the crossroads where he now found himself, providing the final piece he needed in order to arrange the mosaic he had sensed hours earlier.

6

Earlier that afternoon, sensing that the heart of the labyrinth lay in Guatemala, Julio had sat down to reread everything from beginning to end. Facing that notebook, its miscellany reminding him of the delightful disorder of children's almanacs, he could isolate the logic behind most of the five elements that made up that eclectic collage: there were encyclopedia entries, family memories, anecdotes from the Central American trip, playful images and literary quotations that he now knew almost by heart. A final series of fragments escaped his classification.

Written in the first person, they didn't have the objective austerity of the encyclopedic entries or the minimalism of the entries about the trip across the isthmus. They seemed more like nostalgic reminiscences. Confused, he tried to understand the role those fragments played within the text. Their tone reminded him of a quote by Juan Rulfo that was included in the dictionary. Perhaps these were unattributed literary quotations. If so, the internet would know their origins. He opened a browser and typed one of the phrases: "Do you hear? Sometimes it's as if the mountain wanted to say something. I'm not surprised. This village is full of echoes." He found nothing, and turned to considering other possibilities. When night came and he'd had no breakthroughs, he decided it would be best to sleep. It was his wife's voice that, hours later, finally gave him the inspiration he needed to continue the search.

"Amajchel," he'd thought he heard her say at midnight.

And as the voice grew more insistent, so did the intuition that earlier had guided him towards those orphaned phrases. Unable to go back to sleep, he walked to the sofa and opened the dictionary, looking for the fragments he had noticed before. The poetic force of one of them again caught his attention: "Childhood memories? What memories can we have, when we were born into fire?" Opening his computer, he typed the phrase as he'd done with the previous one, but this time he saw the quotation appear in a couple of results. The title of one of them sounded familiar: *A theatre for memory*.

It had been Marie-Hélène's voice at midnight that had led him to the article he now had before him, and she emerged again now that he thought he was finally getting close to the secret meaning of those pages. Trying to distract himself from her image, Julio went back to the quote that he'd recognised mid paragraph: "Childhood memories? What memories can we have, when we were born into fire?" This was not a literary quotation, but rather one of the testimonies uttered in that unusual theatre.

Julio thought it was towards those voices that Aliza wanted to direct him. The flickering flames of those testimonies had marked the path to follow in the middle of the snowstorm. A different voice, pointing in the opposite direction, stopped him.

"What do *you* know?" Aliza had written.

Facing the window beyond which the storm was receding, the question returned to him, now pronounced not by his old friend, but by his wife.

"What do *you* know?" he felt Marie-Hélène reproaching him in the same tender but judicious tone he'd heard ten days earlier.

She was right: of all the characters in the story, he was the only one who refused to appear onstage, the only one who fearfully hid away. With all those voices coming back from his past, he knew the hour had come to act. In the early morning hours, the face before him took on the weight of a summons and a destiny.

Do you hear? Sometimes it's as if
the mountain wants to say something.
I'm not surprised. This village is
full of echoes. And even so, what
I need most is the silence
of the mountain. My father always
told us that that was what the
soldiers had taken away. Nature
wrapped us up like a mother does
her children. And in that silence,
birds sang and animals squealed. Then
came the city and its suffocating commotion
as if they were trying to use noise to
silence the turmoil of their dirty
consciences. I can tell you: the morning
they came to kill my father, the
mountain took me in.

image , ineffable, __infancy__, indefensible

Infancy:
From Lat. "infantia", meaning
"inability to speak".
        From Lat. "in", meaning "no"
        and Lat."fare-/fant",meaning
        "to speak".

—

Each sluggish revolution of the world
Leaves its dispossessed-heirs neither
Of things past nor of those impending.
        —Rilke, "Seventh Elegy"

7

The fox had appeared towards the end of the night, when there was just the first hint of dawn. Julio saw it where he had before: beside the bushes of the neighbour's house. It went to and fro from the steps to the garage, the only movement on the blank slate of the now-frozen landscape. It was hard to know what the animal was looking for in its anxious investigation, but it didn't matter: the essential thing was to surrender to its wanderings as though reading allegories in the still-fresh snow. Two houses down, someone had turned on the first light. Soon day would come and the fox would disappear again.

Julio looked at the clock. It would already be noon in Paris. Trying to think of something other than Marie-Hélène, he returned to the couple of photographs that the news article had included under the image of Juan de Paz Raymundo in profile. He saw the mountain the man mentioned. A slope with trees and grass like any other. Empty land where it was hard to imagine a village had once existed. In the distance he made out the theatre: an imposing structure with a triangular roof, it rose up, solitary on the mountainside. *"Do you hear? Sometimes it's as if the mountain wants to say something. I'm not surprised. This village is full of echoes,"* he remembered having read in the dictionary. The phrase that had caught his attention earlier that day illuminated the image to perfection.

Humahuaca, Cincinnati, Amajchel: it was strange to trace the unexpected equivalence between the three deserts. Julio tried to imagine the play of correspondences that he had just sensed, but he could only call up the image of a young Yitzhak Abravanel, looking out towards the snowy mountains of Zermatt, listening to the tale that led from Karl-Heinz von Mühlfeld to Juvenal Suárez. Having glimpsed the path to follow, he looked outside: a light and graceful snow was falling on the street, and it seemed to him that to watch the snow is always to watch it twice. A return to a distant childhood of which we have no memory.

PART THREE

Theatre of Memory

Maybe a language for endings
demands the total abolition of other languages,
the impassive synthesis
of razed lands.
Or perhaps the creation of a speech of interstices
that would bring together minimal spaces
glimpsed between silence and word
and unknown particles free of avarice.

Roberto Juarroz , "We Have no Language for Endings"

I

Someone, perhaps Juan de Paz himself, had left the window open and let the sparrows in. The birds' flight through the hall, which is as enormous as it is cold, traces the itinerary of a possible description. They come in through the back right window, fly up to the vaulted ceiling of the palm roof, plunge down to the central table that is full to overflowing with architectural models, old magazines and photographic negatives, before passing along the sides of a room reminiscent of a forgotten laboratory, flanked as it is by two giant black blackboards on which are written, in impeccable handwriting, a dozen quotations that it would be good to read carefully right now, except that the sparrows, impatient and playful, return to their eager travels, soaring upwards and then flitting down to perch briefly on the floor covered in old newspapers, where coffee stains alternate with the droppings of those very birds that now fly back out through the window that saw them arrive, first flying over, in passing, a painting that hangs at the back of the room beside two identical black-and-white photographs of a village in ruins. Then, returning to its initial stillness, the space begins to take on a peculiar density that recalls the inside of a shipwreck, where time has been frozen for decades.

Our gaze can then finally come to rest, relax, and read some of the quotes that adorn the blackboards. Latin, Spanish, and K'iche' alternate capriciously in the mosaic:

"*Non est intelligere sine fantasmate.*"

"*Unb'ie' Kul tetzik akunb'ale' ukab'ale' vekat tze'i.*"

Further down, in lines connected to the previous ones by a series of arrows, part of a poem is copied:

> *About suffering they were never wrong,*
> *The Old Masters: how well they understood*
> *Its human position: how it takes place*
> *While someone else is eating or opening a window*
> $\qquad$ *[...]*
> *In Breughel's Icarus, for instance: how everything turns away*
> *Quite leisurely from the disaster.*
>
> $\qquad\qquad\qquad$ W. H. Auden, "Musée des Beaux Arts"

Lines that urge us to stop reading and glance back towards the painting that impassively overlooks the room. The painting – at the bottom of which is a gold plaque with the inscription *Landscape with the Fall of Icarus* – depicts an apparently anodyne scene: a farmer, a shepherd and a fisherman with a rod are going about their tasks under the beating sun, while in the distance ships are heading out to sea. In one corner of the landscape, the painter has included the flailing legs of poor Icarus in his tragic fall. Placed between the two photographs of the village in ruins, the image seemed to corroborate the poet's words: the world continued blindly on its way, indifferent to other people's suffering.

*

Our gaze would like to linger there, to really take in the complex reality of the disaster Breughel's painting narrates with such restraint, except that the sparrows again invade the hall with their flight, and our eyes, always easy prey for distraction, again turn to follow them in their adventures, convinced that as the birds wheel around they are tracing a secret language in the air. And thus, Julio lets himself be carried along by the aerial somersaults of those birds that are now flying over the hall again, stirring up the stagnant time, carrying small flowers in their claws as offerings, as if this were about bringing new air to a house where the fragile silence is sporadically interrupted by brief murmurs that bring to mind old, useless conversations. In this second pass, the sparrows' route disdains the ceiling and they choose to stay close to the ground, as if seeking traces of the absent owner. First they hop on the wicker chair that stands empty and alone, then approach the mattress where, surely, the man who has just excused himself to go to the bathroom sleeps at night. Beside the cot, among rusty tools and what look like broken radio pieces, he glimpses a coffee cup and a half-eaten dish of maize that the birds peck at for a few seconds, before taking flight again and perching on a couple of cork noticeboards.

Hung on the back of each of the main doors, the boards display photographs, newspaper clippings, articles and flyers. An attentive eye might distinguish how news items about the legal proceedings against General Efraín Ríos Montt alternate with forensic reports and flyers for protests. An obituary for Alicia Abravanel, signed by the Artist Commune of Humahuaca, is mixed in with an amalgam of papers that in another instance would have made anyone think of a police station or a detective series.

But birds can't read.

Restless, they flutter up again to disappear down the two side corridors off the back of the hall that give the impression the space goes on indefinitely. Back there is the source of the murmurs that every once in a while flow up towards the hall, only to dissipate and leave it cold and silent, as now. Then, to avoid the claustrophobia of that world full of echoes, Julio has no choice but to look out of the windows, surrender to the promise there: the power of nature in all its splendour, pulsating at midday, covering the mountain with a green blanket that makes it seem like a pleasant garden. It is tempting to get distracted, to imagine possible escapes and possible leisure. But just when he thinks he's found something like peace, there again rises up the memory of the village that had once been there, and with the memory arise the sparrows that, tired of playing in the dark back galleries, now return to the light, carrying with them the whispers of anonymous voices that awaken the five impeccable Labradors that lie splayed out on the floor. Then, finally, he appears. With a simple gesture he calms the dogs, then goes to sit in the empty wicker chair.

2

Julio thought he looked like a tired king, lost in the maze of echoes that he himself had patiently built. Surprisingly tall but bent by the weight of the past that he carried, imperious but empire-less, he alternated between various forms of resentment, timidity, passion and exhaustion. He was wearing a frayed white cotton shirt with a collar embroidered in colourful patterns, over which lay a beaded necklace. The light that shone in through the back window emphasised the scar that ran across his left eyebrow almost down to his mouth, where at times there was the suggestion of a smile that never fully arrived, or that disappeared as soon as it came, as if he distrusted any kind of friendship. A king whom no-one had told the war was over, Julio thought to himself, as he watched Juan de Paz Raymundo get to his feet again, pick up his coffee, and skirt the dozing dogs to cross the hall.

"Do you know the story of Simonides of Ceos?"

He pointed to an old portrait hung on the cork board: a blond man with wavy hair and a severe face, dressed in ancient courtly garb, was depicted there in mid gesture. Further down on the same page someone had written: *Simonides of Ceos, Greek poet,* c. 556 BC–468 BC.

"Apparently he was a poet," replied Julio with a laugh.

"Don't get clever with me, Gamboa. You want me to tell you . . . how the theatre began, right?"

At times Juan seemed to pause mid sentence and rewind what he had said as though checking for mistakes, as though avoiding a stutter. His hands stopped their anxious waving, as if he'd finally lowered his guard, and Julio thought he glimpsed, behind the masks, the face he had seen in photos.

Reading the handful of articles he'd found about Juan and his project, he had the impression of a man of short stature who would be cautious and discreet. Now that they were face to face, he could see his mistake. Juan must have been only thirty-five, but his face showed the maturity of a much older man, and his voice betrayed the distrust of those who have been abandoned. He'd been orphaned at five by the war, the aftershocks of which seemed to be all around them, and he'd spent his life forging his own path. After the village was destroyed, he went to live with an uncle in Guatemala City, but a decade later the uncle decided to migrate north, leaving Juan adrift again. A son of violence, he'd found a family in the Mara Salvatrucha gangs that in those days, after the great waves of deportation following the Chapultepec peace accords, were starting to take over the streets.

For five years, the street offered a way to vent his rage, until one afternoon those same men he would have been willing to die for decided there was no room for an Indian like him in their ranks, and they resolved to beat that knowledge into him. He was saved by a priest who was passing by just as the thugs were about to finish him off. As luck would have it, the

Jesuit knew one of the gang members and convinced him to let Juan live. He was close to death when he heard them walk away, and their cries of "Indian bastard" brought back traumatic childhood memories.

"There's no escaping violence," he told Julio.

And he was right. From those hard years he retained the deep scar that crossed his face diagonally and the striking tattoo that covered his chest and back entirely, until it tangled up like a baroque snake at the base of his neck. He was also left with the dark voice, faltering but serene, of one who knows himself to be a survivor. That voice now went on to tell Julio how the theatre began.

The story of the Theatre of Memory started with an anecdote that was told about the Greek poet Simonides of Ceos. One night, at a banquet sponsored by a nobleman from Thessaly named Scopas, Simonides was invited to declaim a lyric poem in honour of his host. He intoned the verses with precision and grace, but he made the mistake of dedicating several lines to the twin heroes Castor and Pollux. The jealous Scopas declared that he would only pay half of what he had promised. Minutes later, someone came to the door asking to speak with Simonides. When he went outside, the poet found no-one there, but he witnessed an earthquake that reduced the house to rubble, killing the host and all his guests. The ruin was so great that families would not have been able to find their loved ones' bodies, if not for the fact that Simonides remembered exactly where they had been sitting. That mental map, the sign of a prodigious memory, would save the unfortunate guests from an anonymous death.

"My art is born of that catastrophe," said Juan de Paz, running his finger over the cork board, tracing the trajectory of what he called *his art*.

He took two sips of coffee, shooed away a bird that had alighted on the cork, and pointed to a pair of images in which Julio could see the shape of two men. The laurel wreaths adorning their foreheads told him they must be Romans. "Cicero and Quintilian," he heard Juan exclaim, and he thought how strange it was to hear this tattooed man, ex-soldier of the Mara Salvatrucha gangs, speak of oratory and mnemonics in the heart of the mountains.

"Laugh all you want, but books saved me," he added, as though guessing Julio's thoughts.

After the beating, he had spent his convalescence in the Jesuit's residence, absorbed in the books that the priest brought him by the dozen; through reading, he was trying to reclaim the years he'd lost to the labyrinths of violence. At first it was only detective novels, but little by little his tastes changed. The beating had made him remember the traumatic childhood he'd tried to leave behind, and he began to feel a need to delve further into his past. It turned out that the priest had collaborated on the recently published report titled *Guatemala, Memory of Silence*, the Historical Clarification Commission's attempt at bringing to light the human rights violations that had occurred during the armed conflict. As a result, his library was overflowing with history books. During those months of recovery, Juan searched those volumes for something that would explain the whirlwind of terror that, sixteen years earlier, had snatched his parents from him.

*

With the cork boards as backdrop, surrounded by the enormous constellation of political flyers, old photographs and news articles displayed there, Juan de Paz Raymundo seemed like a man caught up in a gigantic historical spiderweb. He waved his arms as if to encompass everything, and his eyes hinted at a deep exhaustion from which he awakened only when, from the rear of the hall, the whisper of voices started up again and reached his ears.

"The theatre's voices keep me on my toes," he said.

As he told it, after three months of recovery he had decided to join forces with the Jesuit. He'd gone on to collaborate with various human rights organisations, mainly helping to translate testimonies.

"They were all Ladinos, people of Spanish descent. They needed people who spoke K'iche'."

He spent his mornings translating the allegations that they hoped someday to use against Efraín Ríos Montt, he said, pointing out a couple of photos where the ex-dictator appeared first as a young man and then older, but always with the same bushy moustache. It was during those years that he had the intuition that would ultimately lead him here, a decade and a half later, to the grasslands of what had once been his childhood village. Confronting hundreds of testimonies that detailed the atrocities carried out by the forces of General Ríos Montt, he had learned that in their determination to depict the abuses committed, historians seemed to forget the more human side of what the conflict meant for many: their everyday memories disappeared behind a blanket of horror that stifled any idle recollection. He himself had felt on more than one occasion that his childhood was a remote realm, separated from him by a high wall of forgetting. And there were many like him: men and women who had been children during the war, and whose memory of life before it was barely a distant rumour. He became obsessed with finding the image behind that curtain of terror.

"It was during those days that I joined the Forensic Anthropology group."

A friend who knew of his preoccupation told him about Clyde Snow and the foundation he had helped create, which sought to resolve cases of human rights violations through the forensic exploration of human remains. What most interested Juan de Paz was the method: the idea of recreating the past from its ruins. He had been part of the group for five years, exploring the mass graves where the terrible truth of the razed villages was hidden. But after a time he lost the taste for it.

"Too much science, too little emotion," he said.

He decided to put that endeavour aside. Unmotivated, he had rambled down various paths of theatre, art and graffiti, until the memory of something he had read during his months of convalescence suggested a road to follow. He remembered that one of the books the Jesuit had lent him had mentioned a long tradition that sought to invoke memories through the construction of mental spaces. The idea of memory as a museum one could peruse on leisurely afternoons struck him as magnificent, capable of animating those recollections that remained hidden after the traumas of war. From that day on he had devoted himself to a tradition that started with the anecdote of Simonides of Ceos and was taken up by Cicero and Quintilian in their attempts to create the art of mnemonics. But it had found its maximum expression in the person and works of the man Juan de Paz Raymundo now turned to.

"You share a name. Giulio, Giulio Camillo, one of the greats."

Julio watched his host point to a hand-drawn portrait of a modest-looking man with a white neckerchief around his neck. Beside the drawing, a handful of images arranged in a semi-circle seemed to show the model for the theatre of memory that had inspired Raymundo's own construction. Further down, as though confirming that intuition, a title page was pinned to the board: *L'idea dell Theatro dell'eccellen M. Giulio Camillo*. "That's where I started," he heard Juan say. Perhaps understanding he was nearing the heart of his story, Juan tossed the dregs of his coffee out of the window and sat back down in his chair, flanked by the dogs that now, roused from their drowsiness, were looking at him attentively.

Distracted, Julio turned his eyes to the two black-and-white photos that rose up behind the man. They showed the ruins of five or six houses not so different from the one in which they sat talking. A couple of children were crouching down and looking questioningly at the camera, while around them flew the ashes of a recent fire. He tried to look for similarities between that razed village and the lush nature around him, but he only managed to revive the memory of some lines he had read weeks before in the dictionary. He patted his backpack to be sure the manuscript was still there, and when he felt it he wondered if this would be a good moment to ask about Aliza Abravanel. He had noticed the obituary tacked to the cork board but decided not to react, instead leaving the floor to this man, whom he imagined as the solitary guardian of a secret he would tell in his own time. But perhaps, he thought as he watched Raymundo pause to play with the dogs, the moment had come to show his cards. To mention the obituary, the photograph, the manuscript that had brought him here. He was preparing to launch into it when he heard the sound of voices start up again from the galleries at the back, and his host began speaking.

"See? The theatre works on a loop."

"How's that?" asked Julio.

"It jolts the memory when you least expect it."

Julio sat looking at him, wondering if this man slept at night, or if the voices woke him in the early morning, dooming him to insomnia. Before him, a handful of mock-ups showed what he imagined were different models of the theatre, whose origins its creator now went on to relate.

The story of Giulio Camillo and his theatre of memory was the stuff of legend. Born at the end of the fifteenth century in Renaissance Italy, Camillo inherited Cicero's and Quintilian's intuition that the world could be reduced to a theatre. And so he dedicated himself to the project that would define his life and even bring him to the courts of King Francis I of France, before whom he would swear, in exchange for patronage, to keep secret that theatre where, it was rumoured, anyone who entered could hold forth for hours on any subject. A wooden theatre, replete with hermetic images and references to the zodiac, by means of which he managed to seduce even Erasmus, in spite of the stutter that plagued Camillo throughout his life.

As Raymundo told it, it had been that mention of stammering that had first caught his attention. For years, he himself had suffered from a slight stutter that only increased when he arrived in Guatemala City at six years old and left behind the K'iche' of his childhood, moving towards a language he still associated with the soldiers who burned his village. At first he had resisted learning Spanish just as intently as he'd once refused to leave that village now in ruins, but the insistence of his uncle, for whom learning Spanish meant survival, eventually won out. The evidence of that imposition had been a stammer, which, even now, years later, sometimes caught him unawares in mid sentence, forcing him to retreat from what suddenly appeared to him as a no-man's-land.

"I know what I want to say, but the words fail me," he said, placing on the table two glasses and a bottle of white rum.

He went on to talk about how, when he'd read about Giulio Camillo and his stammer, he had felt himself reflected in the man. Little did he care that more than five centuries and an ocean lay between them. At the end of the day, they were both men doing battle with expression, searching for methods to revive memory where the spontaneity of words foundered. He set to reading everything he could find about that Renaissance gentleman and his enigmatic project: he read of Camillo's attempts to imagine the theatre as a microcosm where all the world's memory was concentrated, and of his attempts to convince Erasmus. He read of Camillo's death, which he had reached without completing the promised written treatise that would testify to how his project worked. An early death that would come before he had shown his theatre to anyone but the king and a handful of men, but after which the fame of his name and work would grow more than ever, shrouded in mystery, until they came to inspire Robert Fludd's Theatrum Orbis, and later Shakespeare himself, whose Globe Theatre was said to be inspired by the Venetian's utopian vision.

But it was another detail that ended up captivating him. In one of the books, he read of how Camillo had been impacted by the work of Hermes Trismegistus and the tradition of hermeticism, leading him to prize, above all, whatever came shrouded in secrecy. During the time Juan had spent with the Forensic Anthropology group and even during the years when he'd helped the priest transcribe testimonies, he had thought it odd how much emphasis the courts placed on discovering the truth, scientific and quantifiable, of an experience that for him evaded any explanation.

"Camillo understood that it wasn't about baring the secret, but rather doing justice to it," Juan said suddenly, as though trying to summarise his point as he filled the two glasses and invited Julio to drink.

That mention of the secret thrilled him, simultaneously providing him with the link that tied this European story to the Mayan tales he had grown up with. The Popol Vuh, he remembered, also alluded to the secret and the need to care for it.

"Have you ever read it? If not, I recommend it. It is, so to speak, our origin myth," he said, handing Julio a copy.

Inspired by his discoveries and tired of trailing behind the slow workings of the government, Juan de Paz had turned to the creation of that chamber of memories where they now stood. He collected as many traces of the village as he could find: posters, clay pots and instruments, old lamps and clothing, the occasional piece of furniture former residents still had around. He had tracked down three or four inhabitants of the razed village, and, when he found them, he'd asked them to remember. Based on the objects, he had started to put together the details of the theatre, where he sought to recreate the space that the soldiers had tried to consign to oblivion the moment they set it ablaze.

"What Camillo understood is that memory is cumulative. Each new detail illuminates a world."

In those days, Juan de Paz had moved back to the lands where the village used to be. He slept in a tent, and his mornings were devoted to construction. He decided that the building would reflect the architecture of the former houses, so his first year was spent collecting palm fronds with which to construct its enormous roof. He didn't ask for any help, nor would anyone have helped him. From afar he looked like a madman or at least a hermit, immersed in a scheme that even the Jesuit considered hare-brained. Unable to find finance, he had put all his own money into the project. He worked on it for three months and then left for the city to earn more, and when he had enough, he went back, determined to continue. Three years passed like that, until one day he stood in the middle of the theatre and felt the first hint of a memory awaken in him, spontaneous and lively.

"I evoked the rhythms of my mother's laughter. No great revelation, just a small sound."

That memory had convinced him the theatre was ready. He

finished cleaning the space and put an advertisement in the national paper the next week, inviting all the old residents who had survived the genocide to visit the theatre and, with his help, to reconstruct the memory of the simple, everyday essence of their village, beyond the violent recollections that threatened to relegate that time to the swamplands of trauma. After some days, he'd received the first calls. Old locals interested in the project, relatives who had thought him dead, friends a little older than him who claimed to recognise him, though he didn't remember them. They were scattered all over Guatemala, but many of them had still made the trip to the theatre, some seeking to recover contact with their lost friend, others hoping to salvage forgotten memories. The idea of the theatre, he explained, was precisely that the visitors' memories would come to form part of its collection. If someone said in the middle of a session that they remembered the shape of the moon above a distant spring dusk, Juan de Paz would make sure that in the next session, the portrait of that evening would appear, drawn on the backdrop.

"The idea, then, is to rebuild the memory of the village as if it were a museum."

He refilled Julio's glass, and pointed the bottle towards the galleries that led off behind him.

"But why am I telling you about it? Better if you go and see it for yourself."

Julio, afraid of what he might encounter in this labyrinth of voices, downed his drink in a shot, and with the alcohol still burning in his throat, he looked warily at Juan de Paz Raymundo and took the first step.

3

On the base of the cupola that arched over the theatre's central stage, he found an engraved quotation: "'This is the account of when all is still in suspense, all is silent and placid. All is silent and calm. Hushed and empty is the womb of the sky' – Popol Vuh." The wood had been carved by a skilled hand. One by one, Julio followed the letters of that circular writing until, reaching the end, he ran into the beginning, and heard the tape recorder also rewind before starting its loop again, flooding the hall with the testimonies he had heard in the background just moments before. Voices like echoes tracing scenes that at first seemed anodyne, trying laboriously to recompose the spectral architecture that seemed to be hidden all around him.

He saw how Juan de Paz Raymundo had built the theatre based on Giulio Camillo's ideas: seven symmetrical aisles divided the seven terraced stands where, instead of an audience, there were the photographs, drawings, newspaper clippings and other mementos that the theatre's creator had gathered around the memory of the village. In addition to those objects, there were a number of animals drawn on the backdrop of the stage that, as far as he could tell, referenced the naguals that were symbols of the deep alliance between man and nature. He tried to remember what his nagual was, but he barely even remembered his zodiac sign. Then the voices distracted him again, returning him to the spectral logic of that space where Spanish and K'iche' were perfectly blended. He let himself be carried along by the voices that rose up again as solitary whispers.

Damn, Juan de Paz, you really do ask dumb questions. No, we didn't have a childhood. What kind of childhood could we have, when we were learning to set traps for the army at five years old? You call me up and ask me to remember. Memories of the village but not the violence, you say. But what can I tell you? We had no childhood. Unless childhood was that madness you're calling history, and its sign was fire. I do remember that. The nights when my uncle, trying to beat back the darkness, would come home exhausted with a bag full of firewood. The clarity of the fire as it grew, devouring the pine little by little. I remember looking at the flickering flames and thinking that not even watching wood burn was an innocent act for us. Childhood memories? What memories can we have, when we were born into fire?

In the middle of the theatre, hanging from a line, a microphone punctuated the scene. The idea, he imagined, was that when the time came and a visitor felt the prickle of memory, they could go up and record their stories. And the recorded anecdotes were later poured into Spanish by Juan de Paz's stammering voice, to then be incorporated into that tape where the K'iche' voices played at disappearing into his translations. Closing his eyes, Julio tried to follow the resonances that marked the passage from one language to another, but he only managed to catch a faint reverberation of the original language, unintelligible but beautiful. Paradoxically, he felt it was a language that moved forward by retreating, and that what in his host's speech could seem like a slight stutter was really nothing but a way of remaining faithful to the untranslatable language that now flooded the hall again, as if they were standing in a medieval church.

The acoustics of the space helped to produce the game of echoes he had been hearing over the course of the afternoon. The stories, emotional but hermetic, spread out through the space, awaking in Julio too the desire to remember. He thought of Juvenal Suárez's voice, remote and incomprehensible, as Aliza must have heard it on her father's tape recorder. He thought back to the diatribe that the last of the Nataibo, refusing to speak Spanish, had left as a will and testament, and, along with it, the dictum that had led von Mühlfeld into madness: "In the passing from one culture to another, something always remains, even if no-one alive can recognise it." The conjunction of those two memories led him to wonder what the theatre would be like once no-one inhabited it. He imagined the murmuring monologues ringing out over the empty stage, indifferently repeating themselves before the hundreds of mute objects that Juan de Paz Raymundo had set up on the stands.

The vision seemed ominously close to an image of oblivion.

Someone in his childhood had told him that to remember meant to bring something back to the heart, and that childish lesson made him feel that von Mühlfeld was wrong: without witnesses there was no memory. Maybe that was what Aliza had understood when she'd left the manuscript to him. That story was asking for a new heir, a final witness.

Trying to shake off those ideas, worried the alcohol was rendering him dramatic, Julio tried to distract himself by studying some of the newspaper clippings placed around the stands. They were everyday stories. Instead of dramatic war-reporting, Juan de Paz Raymundo had featured a dozen articles about the most ordinary news stories that had occurred during the years of armed conflict: weather reports, football matches, local and international news, over which he had superimposed a collage of images of the village just as it looked now. Julio recognised the mountain where he had walked that same morning with his host, those fields where the dogs ran freely and the memory of violence seemed to recede with the incursion of nature. He had come there looking for an explanation, an ending for the story Aliza had set out before him like a jigsaw puzzle, only to find a clearing in the middle of the woods and the ghosts of that voice that now started over once again.

Remember us. Do not forget us. Do not sweep us away. You shall surely see your homes and your mountains where you will settle. Thus let it be so. Go therefore, go to see the place from whence we came.

Phrases from the Popol Vuh and the Chilam Balam were scattered in among the testimonies. Short quotations briefly punctuated the recording as epigraphs, to later disappear behind their anonymity.

*

Do you hear? Sometimes it's as if the mountain wants to say something. I'm not surprised. This village is full of echoes. And even so, what I need most is the silence of the mountain. My father always told us that was what the soldiers had taken away. Nature wrapped us up like a mother does her children. And in that silence, birds sang and animals squealed. Then came the city and its suffocating commotion, as if they were trying to use noise to silence the turmoil of their dirty consciences. I can tell you: the morning they came to kill my father, the mountain took me in.

Two side windows, half open, let in the light that illuminated the space. There were no lamps in the theatre at all. Feeling slightly claustrophobic, Julio looked outside and thought of Aliza, of Humahuaca, and the unexpected correspondence that linked this mountain to the desert he had recently left. He remembered the map that Walesi and Escobar had built as a memorial on the plains of northern Argentina. He imagined them trying to reconstruct that work every year, only for the summer storms to destroy it, and the image brought him back to this theatre that Juan de Paz, like Sisyphus in his eternal endeavour, was tenaciously building to fight oblivion.

In front of him, five wooden models illustrated the advances of his titanic endeavour. Each bore a date of construction, the first from a year and a half ago, the latest just last month. Julio could see the progress. While the first mockup was just a rough depiction of a couple of generic houses, the latest representation became a detailed map of what the village had been. He saw the houses, labelled with the names of their former inhabitants; the small areas for playing and cooking; the entrance to the village; and even animals grazing in nearby fields. The inhabitants were represented by tiny football-player dolls that reminded him of childhood afternoons when, elbows on the floor, he had played imaginary games with a handful of figurines his father had brought him from Argentina. He wondered if he would be capable of reconstructing the neighbourhood of his own infancy with the same precision as the village depicted here, but when he tried, he only managed to evoke the smell of earth on a rainy day. Then he understood the difficulty that besieged Juan de Paz's project: given the plasticity of memory, the models would proliferate as more and more details were remembered.

In the three most recent models, marking off the boundary of the village, he recognised the contours of the river his host had shown him that afternoon. They had walked for a quarter of an hour, until, descending a slope, the dogs had heard the whisper of the water and taken off running. They had sat down to rest there awhile, while Juan de Paz explained the past of the village before the war.

Listening, Julio was reminded he was a late arrival to this story.

During the walk he had tried to avoid thinking of Aliza, instead concentrating on specific and pragmatic details, but his host's tale had made him think of the shadow young Abravanel had cast over these lands more than thirty years ago. He imagined her, wearing a defiant expression and a camera around her neck as she travelled these settlements caught up in war.

He was a latecomer, but he *had* come, even if all that remained was the memory of what had been.

Listening to the water, he remembered the small river drawn alongside the photograph he had seen in San Antonio de los Cobres, an image that placed Aliza, smiling beside Raúl Sarapura and the greyhound, on the salt flats. "The trick, then, would be to learn to pass from one bank to the other without ceasing to speak." He remembered the quote written in the margin of the drawing, a citation that reappeared in the manuscript he had stowed away in his backpack. He thought about taking it out and offering it to Juan de Paz. Acting as a mere messenger and setting off northwards again. Looking at the man, he knew that to do so would be to repeat the cowardly gesture that had separated him and Aliza years before. If he had come this far, it was in order to go deeper and find the end of the enigma that had been Aliza. To find her there where he had lost her before. His journey, he understood, was a journey of mourning, a private way of coming to terms with the memory that now, three hours later, seemed to well up along with those voices fighting back against oblivion.

When I was a little girl I used to go to the river with my mother. She and the other women went to collect jutes, and I played in the river's current. I also played a game where I tried to grab hold of the fish that slipped away in the water. I'd forgotten that until today. I saw the image of the river in the stands, alongside my mother's old earthenware pots, and suddenly I remembered her singing with her friends. We would get there early to avoid the afternoon rains, and by ten in the morning we'd be back. In those two hours I was always at my happiest. I've also remembered, now, that it was there by the river where the army entered. It was morning, almost dawn . . .

The tape continued, and he heard Juan de Paz's voice interrupt to chastise the witness for that evocation of violence. Julio felt uncomfortable, as if he were unwittingly butting into an argument between strangers. It was odd to be there amid those intimate confessions, to meddle in experiences so far removed from his own life.

He tried to escape the unease by exploring the stands. Beneath the images and objects was an archive of small filing cabinets labelled with various subjects. He opened one that bore the word "Secret", and inside found about fifty index cards similar to those featured in Aliza's *Dictionary*. He picked one up and read.

I remember one day, sometime in 1979, when two ladinos came through the village. They were lost, or maybe exploring. They asked my father for directions. He knew Spanish from the years he'd spent working at the plantation on the coast. I remember watching them in awe, thinking they were speaking a secret language I couldn't understand. As if they were speaking a secret tongue that was the language of adulthood and power.

On the back of the card, a quotation accompanied the testimony:

We have revealed our secrets to those who are worthy. Only they should know the art of writing and no-one else.

There were hundreds more like that. Cards stored in dozens of drawers built into the feet of the stands. Turning the one he held in his hand, Julio read the testimony again while behind him he heard the tape continue to turn, and what he read became confused with what he heard. He had the impression he'd seen this before. Ever since Olivia Walesi's letter had arrived, he'd had the feeling he was living inside a Russian doll, slowly approaching a vast centre that he could now feel close at hand.

He shivered. To the right of the stage, a broken window had been partially covered with a couple of rubbish bags. Juan de Paz had told him hours earlier about the time when one of the witnesses, enraged, had thrown a clay pot at the window through which a cold wind now blew.

"He called me crazy and went running out."

He had a point, thought Julio. That space, with its jumble of whispers and sounds, functioned at the edge of schizophrenia. Even he felt his mind flickering. Unable to concentrate, he was starting to see patterns everywhere. When he'd entered the theatre he thought he'd glimpsed, among the hundreds of objects there, more and more traces of Aliza: a couple of newspaper articles that he thought he'd seen before among the pages of the dictionary; a letter torn in half; a way of putting together words and images that was very particular to her.

Now those coincidences seemed to be multiplying. First it was the familiarity of a couple of testimonies he thought he had read elsewhere, then those cards so like the ones Aliza had used in the dictionary, and he'd just noticed Wittgenstein's eyes amid the stands. He thought he saw connections, vestiges that seemed to corroborate the intuition that had led him there, but it only made him feel penned in by delusion.

On his way there, Julio had thought of a thousand different ways to explain his visit to Juan de Paz Raymundo. He was worried he would be seen as an interloper. He planned to mention the trip Alicia Abravanel had taken through that region years before, and the manuscript that was forcing him to retrace her steps. He intended, even, if necessary, to tell the whole truth: that he was making the trip to free himself from the guilt of having left it unfinished three decades before. To his pleasant surprise, none of those excuses were necessary. Juan de Paz had welcomed him with the same professionalism with which he welcomed the handfuls of tourists who sometimes came to the theatre thinking it was a museum. Recently, the government had built a road that passed nearby on its way north, and the number of visitors had increased. He'd realised that that was his only method of survival: collecting eight hundred quetzales from every gringo who accidentally stumbled on the theatre. With that money he would be able to maintain the place, add some pieces, feed the dogs. That explained why, on seeing Julio arrive, Juan de Paz hadn't asked any questions. And that was why, now that Julio was seeing small traces of Aliza everywhere, the normal thing would have been to feel happy. Without stating his intentions, without having to give explanations, he saw his suspicions corroborated.

But he didn't feel happy.

He felt he was in a trap, like a detective who realises too late that the rigour of his own logic has led him straight into an ambush. Cornered in that world of unpredictable resonances, he felt he was becoming delirious. He tried to calm down by focusing in on the image of Wittgenstein he'd just caught sight of in the stands. There it was, identical to the one in the dictionary: the same face cut in half, the mouth turned to stone, the mute expression of someone stifling a scream. He tried to remember the tranquil afternoons he had spent exploring the eccentric man's life, but he only managed to call up the image of a few deer escaping through the snow.

You, Juan de Paz, have you turned that gadget on? Okay, let's try. I don't know if you'll remember, or if you were too young, but it was in those days that we started to use the traps. Or we had always used them, but against the rats that ate our maize. It was around '79 or '80 when we started to use them against the army. I was just a kid, like you. Six or seven years old. I'm ashamed to say it, but the truth is I thought it was all a bit of fun. I liked the idea of those invisible traps that no-one but us knew about. It was our secret. Soldier fishing, we called it, and I started to think that the whole business was a little like a game. A few months ago the tribunal summoned me to make a statement against Ríos Montt and I imagined myself there, facing all those men in ties, talking about the traps.

The voice faded and the witness started to laugh. A brittle and sincere laugh that bounced around the theatre to reach Julio where he sat in the middle of the stands. A playful but deep peal of laughter that made him think of how, in Aliza's manuscript, von Mühlfeld had cackled nervously as he destroyed the tapes with Juvenal Suárez's recorded voice. He remembered how in that scene, a redheaded nurse witnessed the act, disconcerted, through a half-open door, and he started to feel just as uncomfortable, indiscreet and impertinent as that young assistant. He again felt the disquiet he'd felt minutes earlier, the awareness of having meddled in a world he would never understand no matter how he tried. A world that wore the armour of a hermetic peal of laughter.

It was a similar disquiet, he seemed to remember now, that years ago had provoked the fight that would ultimately separate him and Aliza. He understood, then, his mistake. He saw the blind spot that had so far obscured the precise memory of what had happened in those days. He had come this far believing his own lie: it hadn't been the timing of the impending semester that had forced him to abandon the trip, as he'd thought; it was something else. That was just the fiction he had told himself and the excuse he had given Aliza. Now, in the presence of those voices that seemed to reproach him for his apathy and impotence, he could distinguish the truth that had been hidden. Back in those days, too, something in him – she called it cynicism; he, timidity – had resisted the idea that it was possible ever to fully understand the pain of others. He was dismayed by the pretension of magnanimity and disinterest with which the young Brit threw herself into a reality that was terribly foreign to her. He had agreed to participate in the trip because he was seduced by its more artistic side, attracted by the resonances that would bring him close to Herzog's long walks. But gradually, the more borders they crossed, he had started to feel that the reality exceeded him, and his good intentions amounted to nothing more than naivety and idealism. He pictured himself steering the Jeep towards the border, and he thought that at last he could reconstruct the contours of the scene he had forgotten until now. He could distinguish the way, with each new stop and each new country, the reason for his trip had grown fainter, until it seemed like pure juvenile foolishness. Aliza's camera, in particular, had seemed unnecessary and senseless. What they were starting to see didn't belong to them, not to them nor to the lens that unflinchingly collected the scenes.

"You were born old and cowardly," Aliza had told him, and the words infuriated him.

Now, as the same feeling of unbelonging came over him, he thought she had actually been right. Maybe it was cowardice that had separated him from Aliza, and maybe it was cowardice that made him feel like an intruder now among the voices. It was time to leave behind the comfort of his own world and throw himself into the unfamiliar. Even so, a second thought, more visceral and genuine, made him feel that no matter how hard he tried, he would never be capable of shaking off that feeling of falsehood and hypocrisy. Maybe it was the same feeling that had led von Mühlfeld to destroy the tapes, and Aliza's father to lock himself up in his fear. He wanted to be home, with Marie-Hélène and her dog, far away from this theatre that showed him his most cowardly side.

The desperate fluttering of a bird interrupted his reflections. It had entered by mistake through the broken window and now was battling to find a way out, terrified and anxious. The hall felt darker and colder than before and seemed enormous, and the poor bird flapped around, stuck in the palm cupola. It chased the faint rays of sun that filtered in through the cracks in the structure, but only managed to produce a shadow play that wasn't out of place amid the theatre's echoes.

Julio left the stands, walked to the window, and opened it wide.

Outside, the afternoon was starting to fade, while in the distance a couple of clouds suggested the remote possibility of a downpour. The hours had passed without him noticing, enveloped in Juan de Paz's stories and the hum of voices that at first he'd believed was perfectly cyclical, but in which he now started to notice certain fluctuations. With each loop, the order of the testimonies changed. Some of the monologues disappeared, and others entered the rotation. Like memory on shuffle, he thought, while he watched the bird flounder among the galleries until it finally found the window. A spiral of memory that at times carried new testimonies, like the one that now found its way to him, then floated out of the window and disappeared down the mountain, imitating the flight of the birds.

For a long time, I could only remember my childhood in dreams. People always talk about fortune tellers who dream the future. The Bible and other books are full of things like that. Prophecies and visions of the future that come in the middle of the night. Me, on the other hand, after the incident – I dreamed of enigmatic images that reached me from the past. Always the same dream, with minimal variations. Without distinguishing the details of the scene, I thought I saw myself in the fields around my village, playing with friends.

All normal up to there.

But the thing is, in the dream the toys weren't toys, they were little disfigured dolls that didn't seem to make sense. I'd get up in the middle of the night feeling like I'd been there, confused and unsettled by the enigmatic scene. In the dream it was simultaneously me and someone else living that experience. It repeated every two or three nights with the insistence of an idée fixe. I'd see us there again, lying on the damp earth, playing with those deformed little figurines. I'd get up in the middle of the night, open my notebook, and start writing.

I tried to reconstruct what I'd seen, incomprehensible as it seemed.

I was frustrated on the one hand at not being able to understand what was happening, and on the other by the feeling there was so much at stake. But we all know oracles speak in enigmas. They say something no-one understands, but that seems to hide a truth. For a time, in the months leading up to the construction of this theatre, I thought that dream was the oracle that would bring me back to my lost childhood. I grew obsessed with it. I kept a diary where I recorded its variations and mutations.

One day I noticed something.

I realised my friends and I weren't the only inhabitants of the dream. There was someone else moving around the space. A figure without a face. A silhouette that little by little took shape in the diary until it became a kind of white shadow over the margins of the scene. That's what I called it – the white shadow – and with that name I tried to exorcise its memory. By then I had already started the initial phase of the theatre project, so I started asking questions of the oldest villagers.

At first they looked at me like I was crazy.

If they didn't already think me mad, they were convinced when I came around asking about that shadow. They thought I was seeing ghosts. So I stopped asking, until finally I thought I saw more. There was one night when I saw, beside us kids, the outline of a woman walking along the river. Then I went back to asking around, and *everyone again looked at me with concern, except for one woman who laughingly remembered that in those days, a young British woman had come through the village. Maybe she was the white shadow. Many people sleep trying to forget. I went towards sleep in search of memory.*

At times the voice stopped and then there was another sound: a sort of scratch or scraping that repeated three or four times. A lighter lighting a cigarette, thought Julio, while he mentally tried to reconstruct the scene: the outline of a man smoking alone in that cavernous space that had much in common with a temple. He heard a deep inhale, and then the voice went on with its story. Inside the theatre, his voice lost the dissonance of his usual stammer and took on a new rhythm.

It's him, Julio thought. They are all him, in a way, but this *is* him. These are his memories.

Julio pictured the man waving his hands before the empty theatre, his voice contending with his emotion. Though Juan de Paz had translated and read many of the testimonies, he thought he could distinguish the gleam of personal memory shining through his words. A certain biographical tinge became clear in the inflections of that voice, forcing Julio to remember the question Olivia Walesi had asked him in Humahuaca when she'd given him the manuscript of *A Private Language*.

"Fiction or memoir?" she had asked.

And Julio had wavered at first. He knew about his friend's conceptual games, the mechanisms by which she sought to confuse the reader. But now, listening to that voice as it left off the cigarette and started speaking again, he thought he understood that if he'd made it this far it was in order to explore that invisible border where fiction blurred into memory. He got the sense that this man had set everything up – the stands, the photographs, the models, the crockery – just so he could bury, amid so much testimony, his true purpose. Juan de Paz had thrown himself into his project with the secret intention of camouflaging the confession Julio was now listening to. A story in which, transformed into a white shadow, he thought he recognised Aliza.

The old woman thought back, and then the memories of the other villagers were kindled. They started to remember things. Details that I collected even when they seemed contradictory. Some said she was British, others American. Some thought she'd been a missionary, and others swore she was some kind of diplomat, maybe from the United Nations. But no-one seemed to remember her name. Sometimes they thought she was blonde, other times brunette. They thought they could clearly picture her walking through the village during those dark days, but no-one could give me a name.

Meanwhile, I went on recording my dreams.

It was in those days that I opened the theatre. I put an advertisement in the paper and waited. A month later, an old friend of my father's called and asked to see me. He came the next week. Mostly he wanted to talk, find out about me, what had become of my uncle. Things like that. It was hard to convince him to go into the theatre, but I did. I told him to do it for my dad. Back then the theatre wasn't what it is now, it was just a dozen drawings, newspaper clippings, an empty model in the middle as a reminder of why we were there. The old man went in without expecting much, but the truth is he got into the game. He recorded some memories of my father that were hard for me to listen to, and some other minor details: the names of old friends, the layouts of some houses, the laugh of an old love.

I took the opportunity to ask about the white shadow.

At first he thought I was talking about the soldiers, but then he seemed to remember. He recalled the British girl, her dark hair and white skin. The kid always had her camera around her neck, he said, and that memory shifted something in me.

I urged him to keep thinking.

He couldn't recall her name, but he came up with one other detail: he said the girl had left her film in town. She'd given it to a distant cousin of hers who lived in the city. I let him talk. He told me again about the memories he still had of my father, but I kept thinking about the lead he'd just given me. Two days later I got the contact information for her cousin, whose name was Itzel, and set out for the city to meet her.

I told her about my dreams and the white shadow that moved at its edges.

I saw her laugh, and something about her laughter soothed me.

Itzel did remember the British girl perfectly well. It was the first time I'd heard of rock music, she told me. She also remembered her camera and photos. To my surprise, she still had the old film the girl had given her. I'm just obsessive, never throw anything out, she told me as she stood up, and, skirting piles of objects, dug through some old boxes until she found a bag with five rolls of film, which she handed to me. Inside the bag, on a slip of yellowed paper, there was a name and a date: Aliza Abravanel, May 19, 1982.

The voice paused again. To take another drag on the cigarette, thought Julio, and he felt that the ambush he had sensed was starting to play out before him. He recognised the date and the film rolls that Aliza had also mentioned in the dictionary. Those words were directed at him. Even so, a second impression made him feel that the voice wasn't talking to anyone but its owner. No matter how much it told, even when the story seemed to bare itself the most and approach a truth, something in it withdrew. This isn't about baring the secret, but about doing justice, Juan de Paz had said to him, and it was a declaration he also remembered reading in the manuscript. He didn't know at what point he'd become trapped in this echo chamber, but he sensed it was too late to escape. There was no point in resisting. He decided to surrender to the correspondences being set up there, let himself be carried along on the currents of a monologue that, like a turbulent river, now pushed him onwards as it dredged up forgotten memories.

For many months, that was all I had: a name, a dream and a handful of film rolls. After some time I gathered up my courage and decided to develop them. Maybe they held the past I was looking for. But no. The years had destroyed them. All that remained was useless tape. So I was left with the name and the dream. I decided to investigate. To find who was hiding behind that name.

Aliza Abravanel.

So many a's alternating in that strange name. I went back to asking among the villagers, but I didn't come up with much. Until someone suggested the obvious solution: I didn't have anything to lose by looking online. They were right: a quick search and her image was before me. She looked older and her name wasn't Aliza, but Alicia Abravanel, but something in the play between her dark hair and white skin made me sure that it was her. I know it sounds strange, but something about that contrast made me sense I was finding the white shadow I had glimpsed in dreams.

I couldn't track down any address, just a detail that gave me a destination.

I read how this woman, who was now a renowned author, lived in an artists' commune on the outskirts of a small village in northern Argentina. So without thinking twice I wrote a letter, which I sent to the commune, thinking maybe once it was there, someone would know how to get it to her. In the letter I talked about the theatre, the film rolls and the village. I told her about the white shadow that appeared in my dream and the strange toys that somehow condensed all the horror of what was to come. I mailed the letter without much hope, like someone sending a message into the future.

Not expecting a reply.

I tried to forget. I threw myself into the theatre's activity, the construction of that project that was growing amid my own confusion. Two months later Jacinto called saying that a letter for me had arrived from Argentina. It was signed by a certain Raúl Sarapura, who said he was working with Abravanel on her final project. He told me she was not in good health, but that she'd received my letter with the utmost enthusiasm. She remembered the village well, Itzel's smile, the rolls of film. Then, strangely, he proceeded to thank me. He told me about the project the writer was spending all her hours on, and the dead end they'd found themselves in. I remember his words exactly, as they struck me as odd and excessive: Your letter, he said, has given Aliza the hope of a solution. He closed that first *message by talking about my dream. He mentioned a Russian novel in which the protagonist remembers a childhood game which consists of two parts. First there is a set of toys, a dozen absurd objects called* nonnons. *Shapeless, bulky objects, twisted or full of holes, somewhat like fossils or sea anemones. Objects that would make little sense on their own, except that an equally illogical and twisted mirror is sold along with them, and when you hold the objects up to it they finally take shape. Suddenly, there is the little elephant, the giraffe or the piglet that everyone has looked for unsuccessfully. I suspect, said Sarapura in the letter's last line, that the toys in your dream work with a similar logic. He signed off with a hug from them both and promised to write again very soon.*

After that letter came many more, but none made me feel what I did that first day. I finished reading beside the river and walked back to the theatre. I sat down in the chair where I am now and started to think about what I had read. I thought of the dream. I tried to imagine the crazy mirror Sarapura talked about, and suddenly I felt like I had it before me. On the wall, where there is now a photograph of a cloudless sky, back then there was a blue brushstroke painted in a short spiral. Some weeks before, I had woken up thinking of the sky of my youth, and suddenly the memory had led me towards a colour. A blue midway between sky blue and indigo, a colour it took me a week to find, but that I finally had. That brushstroke was there as testament to my seemingly useless memory. I remember how that afternoon, thinking of Abravanel's letter, I sat looking at that blue brushstroke. And suddenly, without knowing exactly how, I felt that the shape of the stroke, that spiral that at first had seemed capricious and spontaneous, combined with the other objects there to evoke a complete memory, up to now forgotten. I remembered the gesture my father made when he finished telling me a story when I was a child. A minimal gesture, a sort of spiral that indicated the end of the tale, but that led me to think of the blue of celestial bodies.

That was the first memory.

One always has the feeling that life is hiding something, a secret cultivated with the patience of a gardener tending his garden. That day I had the sense that with my first memory, I was getting close to the secret I had cultivated for years. More memories came later. As if behind that gesture of my father's was hidden the uncanny mirror the letter had mentioned. As if in the conjunction of that colour and that shape, that particular blue and that gesture, the lost memory could be found.

And thus I could remember.

I remembered my father's taciturn, severe face, the cracks in the damp earth on rainy days, the sound of the Montezuma pine as it burned, the bare legs of the women wading into the river, a pair of old shoes stored in a corner like a novelty brought from far away, these mornings that I've now seen again, the incense scent of copal, the time I got lost for long minutes out on the mountainside, our joy as we played with our toy cars, the marbles my uncle brought from one of his trips to the plantation, the raccoons that besieged the milpas and the traps we set to protect the crops, the confusion and fear I felt the day I saw the first rifle, my parents curled up in bed in positions I didn't understand, a couple of dogs gnawing corncobs while we heard the birds circling over the mountain, the catechism lessons, the useless pleasure I discovered the first time I took a branch and scratched a drawing into the riverbank, the twinge I felt the first time I entered the capital, my uncle's drunken face as he shouted, ironic in his suffering, Viva Guatemala, viva la Patria, a squirrel

*hanging from a branch and the impression that the branch would
break at any moment . . .*

The list went on, marking the rhythms of a litany in which the very precision and clarity of memory risked making it inscrutable, opaque and anonymous. Impossible to exhaust experience. Absolute memory is very much like forgetting, thought Julio, while he noticed how the light was gently fading, insinuating the arrival of evening. He thought he heard a bark, but couldn't make out whether the sound came from the recording or reality. Overwhelmed by so much detail, fearful that night would find him there, he told himself it was time to leave this limbo where he had now found Aliza again, converted into a white shadow. He left behind the voice that went on with its enumeration of memories, and as he went out through the theatre's main door, he saw Juan de Paz. His host seemed energised by the cup of coffee he was drinking, and had returned to the nervous, bustling state in which Julio had first found him.

"I'll be right with you," he heard him say.

On the table, the bottle of alcohol was right where they had left it. He poured a shot and downed it quickly, perhaps seeking to shake off the suffocating vision he thought he'd just had. He quietly picked up his backpack, excused himself by saying he needed a little air, and, patting the dogs, went out through one of the back doors.

4

Sensing the arrival of dusk, the sparrows had disappeared, their acrobatic flights replaced by the freezing wind that blew over the mountain towards the river and died down where the hill descended, under the half moon that was just starting to emerge. Julio's eyes followed the effect of those gusts over the damp grass. Maybe because of the alcohol, he found a certain peace in the lightness of those winds that caressed the grass as if an invisible presence were moving over the brush.

It was hard to imagine that a village had once been here.

He thought of the voices in the theatre, the contrast between the claustrophobic game of echoes in there and the free, unlimited expanse of the field he now walked through. A second idea, fanciful and mad, made him doubt the first. He felt that the voices he had just heard extended out over the mountain, and that Juan de Paz Raymundo had built a theatre that threatened to encompass all. He remembered that one of the Kafka texts he had given Aliza when they were young – he couldn't remember which – spoke of a limitless theatre of life where every gesture unfolded outward in the act. The Nature Theatre of Oklahoma, he remembered aloud, and felt his words reverberate as if he were still sitting in the stands, listening to the testimonies he'd just left behind.

A theatre more real and powerful than reality itself.

That afternoon, sitting before the cork boards and listening to Juan de Paz talk about the origins of his project, he had suspected that that was the secret ambition hidden behind it all: a desire to convert the present into a simple déjà vu. Now he understood that the man had been successful.

He tried to reconstruct the image of the village according to what he'd seen in the models. He situated the houses, the animals, the areas of play and agriculture, he even tried to recognise the layout in the two photographs of the village in ruins that flanked the Brueghel reproduction. He managed to reconstruct a very basic portrait of the village, a sketch of what it could have been, but another cold gust ran over the mountain, and along with the cold he felt the image disappear. The strange thing, he thought, was this: all the other villagers came, visited the theatre, remembered what they needed to remember and then left, hopeful that the unusual exercise would help them exorcise the traumas that tied them to an unfinished past. They came, remembered, and forgot. They went on with their lives, while Juan de Paz would stay there, locked in a theatre that barred his path to forgetting.

Trying to escape the cold and those bottomless thoughts, he decided to walk in the direction of the wind, towards the river. Backpack in hand, protected by the alcohol that was still warming his body, he went back along the road he'd walked that afternoon with Juan de Paz and his dogs, until, descending the hill, he could hear the rushing of the water. Apparently it had rained up on the mountain, and now the water was rougher and more turbid than it had been hours earlier. He remembered the testimonies evoking memories of things that had happened along that riverbank, the mornings the old inhabitants had spent there. He wondered just what were those creatures called *jutes* that were mentioned so often. The army had entered from there, one of the voices said before Juan de Paz interrupted. And it had been that slip-up and interruption that had led him to remember the reason for the fight he'd had more than thirty years ago with Aliza.

But it didn't matter.

His clear cowardice was in the past. The important thing was to have come here, even if it was late. To know how to experience the consequences of what had begun then.

"The Greeks," Juan de Paz had told him hours earlier, "had two rivers: one for forgetting and the other for memory. Lethe and Mnemosyne."

He tried to recreate the scene he'd just heard in the theatre. He imagined the children lying on the grass playing with toys that in the dream became enigmatic, while around them the white shadow that was Aliza smiled. Now he understood that she had constructed the dictionary around that particular scene. He took it from his backpack now and flipped through the notebook until he found the page he was looking for.

On May 19, 1982, I decided to leave Guatemala. I was carrying with me the film rolls I had taken on April 15. I thought about developing them, sending them to some newspaper as a testament to what I'd seen. But somehow I felt that the world was already full of images, and the photos would not be enough to do justice to what I'd seen. I took the rolls and gave them to a distant cousin in the city and told myself that from that day on, I would only write, like someone searching for the caption of an impossible photograph.

There again was the white shadow of the dream, hiding behind the flash of an absent photograph. Aliza and Juan de Paz had collaborated, planning out the perfect trap that had led him here. He laughed as he realised how naive he'd been, thinking all this time that he was the one carrying the message, when the real message was for him. It would have made little sense to give those papers to a man who could have recited them by heart.

He remembered the photograph at the start of the story that had led him here, that image of Karl-Heinz von Mühlfeld alongside Juvenal Suárez, in front of the ruins of Elisabeth Förster-Nietzsche's old mansion. Something that started there was ending here, on this mountain where every occurrence seemed to be the reverberation of some long-forgotten event. He looked to the sky in search of relief, but the image of Yitzhak Abravanel, alone on the streets of New Germany, emerged again. He was afraid of becoming just another character in that theatre, unable to put the final stop to a work that threatened to become omnipresent.

What would Marie-Hélène say, as an architect, about that space where the voices rang out anonymously, advancing towards a past that recoiled? He thought of the models that lay in the darkness of the house he had left, and of the wanderings of the fox he had followed on the night of the storm. More than once during those solitary days, sitting in the living-room and gazing out of the window, he had tried to find patterns in the still fresh snow: small castles, improvised archipelagos, mazes the fox navigated at will, determined to build a home in the elements. Now, facing that swollen river, he wondered if the snow would still be there on his return, or if time would have destroyed the cartography he had imagined so patiently.

He turned and looked back towards the theatre, but all he saw was the mountain slope. Vast, rebellious and fierce, the fields grew without memory, incapable of knowing that they had unintentionally erased the violent traces of all that had happened there. Aliza had walked through those same fields. Julio thought he saw her, the camera around her neck and her eyes defiant, aware that what she was seeing eluded anything the camera could capture.

The sound of the water, ever more tempestuous, brought him back to the present. Pounding and indomitable, nature would end up turning even the most impressive fortress into a graceless ruin. In the distance, he made out the road that had brought him there. Years later, he imagined, a family on vacation would cross that road on their way north, and, passing by that mountain, would glance out of the window at the solitary theatre overgrown with weeds. They would wonder who had lived there, never imagining that Juan de Paz Raymundo had built that space precisely as a brief refuge against ruin.

"Like a house in the desert," he'd said with a laugh hours earlier, words that could only take Julio back to Humahuaca.

Looking around him, Julio realised he was right. The beauty of his achievement lay in its bold ambition. Like Aliza, Juan de Paz sought to build a mausoleum in which to bury the secret of an unjust past. Anxious, Julio patted his backpack, making sure the other manuscript he carried was also safe.

Earlier that day, one of the dogs had dug a hole beside the river. He took the two manuscripts out, bound them together with an elastic band, and unceremoniously buried them, then covered the mound with a pile of leaves. Tomorrow at the latest, the dog would come back there and nose around until it found them, and it would exhume the pages that smelled of earth. The buzz of insects eventually convinced him it was time to return. Night was advancing steadily over the mountain. Lighter now, his backpack empty, he went back down the path until, reaching level ground, he could see Juan de Paz through one of the windows. Frenetic, he seemed to be floundering among ghosts, far removed from the sunset that would soon sink him into darkness. Sheltered, thought Julio, by the glow of a fixed idea and the incandescence of memory.

ACKNOWLEDGEMENTS

They say that writing is a solitary profession. It is, but sometimes it's a crowded solitude. I have rarely felt as supported as when I was chasing down the elusive traces of the characters who appear in these pages. The book would not have been possible without the help of Ignacio Acosta and Claudia Guerra, who imagined and recreated the *Dictionary of Loss*. Nor would it exist without the readings, enthusiasm, and suggestions of the unfaltering Sandra Pareja and the team at Massie & McQuilkin. I must thank four people in particular for making this translation a reality: Megan McDowell, Julia Ringo, Bill Swainson and Katharina Bielenberg. Thanks to each of them for showing me the powers of editing and for being the most attentive, generous and perceptive readers. The same goes to Silvia Sesé and Linus Guggenberger, readers of the early versions of the novel, who helped make it better.

CARLOS FONSECA was born in Costa Rica in 1987, brought up in Puerto Rico and studied in the USA. He was selected by the Hay Festival as part of the *Bogotá 39* group (2016), by *Granta* magazine as one of its list of the twenty-five best young Spanish-language writers (2021) and by *Encyclopaedia Britannica* as one of the twenty most promising writers in the world for their 'Young Shapers of the Future' (2022). His previous novels are *Colonel Lágrimas* and *Natural History*, both translated by Megan McDowell. His work has been translated into English, German, French, Italian, Greek, Turkish and Croatian. He is a lecturer in Spanish at Trinity College, Cambridge.

MEGAN MCDOWELL has translated many of the most important Latin American writers working today, including Mariana Enriquez, Samanta Schweblin, Alejandro Zambra and Lina Meruane. Her translations have won the English PEN award, the Premio Valle-Inclán, the O. Henry Prize and most recently the National Book Award, and have been nominated for the International Booker Prize (four times). Her short story translations have been featured in the *New Yorker*, *Paris Review*, *New York Times Magazine*, *Tin House*, *McSweeney's* and *Granta*, among others. In 2020 she won an Award in Literature from the American Academy of Arts and Letters. She is from Richmond, Kentucky and lives in Santiago, Chile.